Dear Reader,

I met the composite of Anna in 1972 at an informal meeting of air force wives. We'd gathered, ostensibly, to discuss the women's movement and our part in it. Soon enough, however, we were talking about how limited we were.

Our husbands' work ruled our lives. Military restrictions dictated the jobs we could hold, the places our families could live, the weight of our possessions during frequent moves. After all had voiced their discontent, the most vehemently dissatisfied of us all stood, held up a hand for silence and said...

"But Mitch makes everything worth it."

Angel Milan

ANGEL MILAN,

author, editor, publisher, freelance journalist, speaker and writing teacher, lives in Silver City, New Mexico. She and her husband, Ted (also a writer with similar credentials), enjoy reading, building more bookshelves (there are never enough), working in the garden and being ruled by their three cats—Tiger Dude, Baby Cass and Patches.

Books by Angel Milan

Silhouette Special Edition

Autumn Harvest #39
Sea of Dreams #200

Silhouette Desire

Snow Spirit #34
Sonatina #64
Summerson #96
Out of Bounds #118
Danielle's Doll #153
Sugarfire #214
Anna's Child #226
Knock Anytime #285

& BACHELORS USA

Angel Milan
Anna's Child

Published by Silhouette Books
America's Publisher of Contemporary Romance

SILHOUETTE BOOKS

ISBN 0-373-82266-9

ANNA'S CHILD

Copyright © 1985 by Angel Milan

All rights reserved. Except for use in any review, the reproduction
or utilization of this work in whole or in part in any form by any
electronic, mechanical or other means, now known or hereafter
invented, including xerography, photocopying and recording, or in
any information storage or retrieval system, is forbidden without
the written permission of the editorial office, Silhouette Books,
300 East 42nd Street, New York, NY 10017 U.S.A.

All characters in this book have no existence outside the imagination of
the author and have no relation whatsoever to anyone bearing the same
name or names. They are not even distantly inspired by any individual
known or unknown to the author, and all incidents are pure invention.

This edition published by arrangement with Harlequin Books S.A.

® and TM are trademarks of Harlequin Books S.A., used under license.
Trademarks indicated with ® are registered in the United States Patent
and Trademark Office, the Canadian Trade Marks Office and in other
countries.

Visit Silhouette at www.eHarlequin.com

Printed in U.S.A.

One

Crack!

Anna jumped and let the heavy suitcase fall from her hand. The screen door hit a second time, the rebound a soft thud, as Anna turned from Germaine Rankin to look back.

"Woo, wooo!"

A three-foot bundle of energy sped toward her with churning arms and flying blond hair. Hands outstretched, he stopped with a bounce against her suitcase, then looked up.

"I'm George Thomas Rankin," the boy said, smiling and panting. He pointed at her. "And you're Anna Harte."

Anna knelt down and extended her hand. "I'm so glad to know you, George Thomas," she said.

"G.T.," he said seriously, giving her hand a strong squeeze. "Nobody calls me George."

"G.T. it is, then. How old are you, G.T.?"

He pulled his hand away and waved four fingers at her. "But I can read and name all the dinosaurs," he said.

"You must study very hard," Anna said.

G.T. curled his fingers around the handle of the suitcase and tried to lift it. It slid forward half an inch on the hooked rug. "Be five in June," he said proudly, releasing the case and wiping his hand on the front of his shirt.

A sharp whistle cut through the air, and G.T. whirled and ran back toward the door. Anna stood, blinked as the door slammed again, then looked at Germaine Rankin. The boy's mother was grinning.

"George doesn't stand on ceremony," she said. "Just blows in and out like a strong wind."

"He's a beautiful child," Anna said.

"Isn't he, though," Germaine said, stepping forward to take Anna's suitcase.

"Woo, wooo!" The screen creaked open, and G.T. was on his way back in. This time he sat atop the shoulders of a tall, dark man who ducked down low so the two of them could clear the doorframe.

"All aboard for the kitchen, the dining room, and points south," the man said.

"We're hungry," G.T. announced, adjusting the cowboy hat that swamped his head and threatened to fall forward over his eyes.

"Men," Germaine said resignedly, but with a smile. "Aren't they always hungry?"

Anna realized she hadn't stopped staring since the two had come through the door. Her survey had started at the man's heavy brown cowboy boots, progressed up long legs clothed in Levi's denim, continued over the light blue work shirt with pearl snaps, and came to an end in the depths of lustrous, twinkling brown eyes. She looked away, toward Germaine, only to look back again, her eyes locking on the large hands that rested lightly over small, corduroy-clad knees.

His fingers were wide, long, and strong-looking, the result of hard work. They were as tan as his face, but a contrasting shadow of black beard made the hands seem gentler than their size would indicate. Tendons flexed as the boy he secured wiggled forward.

"Take it easy, partner," the huge man said to the tiny child. "You'll bust this ole bronco for sure."

"There'll be plenty of time for riding later," Germaine said. "Get out of the saddle and get washed up for supper, G.T."

G.T. held on to the hat as the man knelt down and swung his young rider to the floor. "You've got your orders, old man." G.T. looked disappointed as the cowboy hat was lifted and replaced on its owner's thick black hair. "I'll be along," the man assured him.

Anna stepped back out of the way as G.T. ran by. She was grateful for the high, mirrored chiffonier beside her. It was a barrier between her and the friendly greetings that were taking place. She'd never expected such a scene to happen in her first few minutes in the previously quiet boardinghouse.

"Come here and give me a hug, you old bronco," Germaine said, swinging her arms wide, then wrapping them around the man. "You're a sight, you are." Several pats on the back later she tugged on his shirt and turned him around.

"Come on, now, I want you to meet someone."

The man looked at Anna as if he hadn't been aware of her presence before. He swiped the wide-brimmed hat from his head and held it belt high while a slow smile of approval spread across his face.

"This is Anna Harte. Anna, my nephew, Mitch McCabe."

Mitch ducked his head slightly as he took a step forward, then offered his hand. "A pleasure, ma'am."

"Anna's from San Antonio."

The roughness of his skin pressed against hers, reaffirming her intuition about hard work. The feel of him gave her pleasure. "San Antonio," Anna repeated without thinking.

"Texas," he said.

Anna nodded, then had to smile. He wasn't making fun of her, she realized, he just wanted to put her at ease. It was time to get rid of the serious look and act as if she were pleased to meet him.

"I'm from Texas, too. Winkler County," he said, still holding her hand. "What brings you to New Orleans?"

"Business." It sounded too stiff for the occasion. "I guess you could say I'm going to school," Anna said, then withdrew her hand from his.

"Anna's a chef down there in San Antone," Germaine said. "She's here to apprentice with Pep over at Lucullan."

"Whew!" Mitch let out a long breath. "That's high class. Pep lays a nice table."

"That's what your aunt was telling me," Anna said.

He winked. "Philippe wishes he could cook as good as she does."

"Go on," Germaine said and cuffed him on the arm.

Mitch tossed his hat toward a wooden rack by the door, hit the rounded spike perfectly, and gave a satisfied nod of his head.

"Haven't lost your touch, have you, Mitch?" Germaine said.

"I've missed a few."

Anna was feeling more out of place every second. It was obvious that these two hadn't seen each other for some time, and she would prefer to be out of their way so they could visit privately. Top of the stairs, turn left, last door on the right. Germaine's directions were repeated in her mind as she lifted her suitcase. She hadn't taken two steps when the weight suddenly disappeared from her hand.

"I'll get that for you," Mitch said.

"I can handle it," Anna said. "I know you and your aunt would like to visit."

"Plenty of time for that," he said. "I'll be staying the month."

Anna frowned. She'd thought Germaine Rankin's boardinghouse was for women only. "You're staying here?" she asked.

"Always do," he said easily.

"I thought..."

"You thought right, honey. Women only," Germaine interrupted. "But we make exceptions for family." She gave a short laugh. "And G.T. kind of breaks the rules, too."

Anna didn't mind having little George around at all; children were her special delight. But she'd planned to get away from all the men in her life. Just because they all happened to be in her own family was of little consequence. The idea was to have a peaceful vacation, to spend a month without a concerned patriarch, an overprotective uncle, or a bossy brother looking over her shoulder.

"Race ya!" George wheeled through a side door and hit the stairs at a run.

Mitch took off right behind him, Anna's suitcase still in his hand. He carried it as if it weighed nothing until G.T. turned to look back at his pursuer. Mitch slowed to a loping walk, the heavy case appearing to make him list to one side. G.T. scrambled on to the top.

"I'm gettin' too old for this racin' up the stairs."

"No you're not," G.T. countered.

Mitch straightened and walked the rest of the way. "Give me a hand here, partner." G.T. curved two fingers under the handle. "You know where we're goin'?"

G.T. nodded, then pointed.

Anna gave Germaine a puzzled look.

"George helped me make up your bed before he went to preschool this morning."

"Oh."

"Things will quiet down tomorrow," Germaine said, her eyes twinkling with good humor. "George hasn't seen Mitch for a year. They're always a bit rowdy the first night."

Anna smiled despite her misgivings. "They must miss each other very much," she said.

Germaine started up the stairs, and Anna stepped up beside her. "Won't be long now till George is old enough to go visit Mitch," Germaine said thoughtfully. "He pesters me about it already, but just thinking about him around all those horses makes me a nervous wreck.''

"I can imagine," Anna said.

"'Course, Mitch would take good care of him, but he's still my baby.''

"You have other children?" Anna asked.

"Two. Both moved away. Grown and gone." Germaine sighed. "George was a surprise."

Anna didn't know exactly what to say. A child born to a woman of Germaine's age could be a godsend or could cause grief, but she seemed a happy person. "A perfectly delightful surprise," Anna said.

"To be sure," Germaine said. "But a handful since George senior passed away."

"I'm sorry," Anna said quietly as they neared the top of the steps.

"Heart trouble. Took him all at once. Neither one of us knew."

Anna thought of her own father, robust, full of energy, such a powerful man. He was the man she most wanted to get away from by coming to New Orleans. "I'm sorry," she said again. "You must get lonely."

"I did at first, but I have my girls now. Full house most of the time."

Anna stopped at the top of the stairs and looked around. "This is a beautiful old house," she said. "It reminds me of my grandmother's."

"It *is* nice, isn't it?" Germaine stopped beside her. "We bought it about seven years ago and started fixing it up. For the grandchildren, you know." She shrugged, then started down the hall to her left. "Makes a perfect boardinghouse, though. Six bedrooms up here, three down, nice big kitchen. You've got the best room in the place. I know you're going to like it."

"I'm sure I will," Anna said.

"Windows side and back. You can look right down into the garden in the backyard...or down on the street if you get bored with watching the plants grow."

"I don't think I'll have much time to get bored."

"Pep will run you ragged if you let him," Germaine said.

"You know Mr. Gutierrez well, do you?"

"He's been a friend for a long time. Philippe Allen François Gutierrez. Best food in town, no matter what you have a taste for."

"With a name like that, I wouldn't doubt it."

"We're lucky that way here in New Orleans. A real American mixture with a flavor all its own. Fine people."

"I'm glad Mr. Gutierrez recommended that I stay here," Anna said.

"So am I, Anna." Germaine stopped in front of a doorway and motioned for Anna to precede her inside.

Anna could hear voices, but there was no one in the room. Neither Mitch nor George had passed them

in the hallway and there was no other way back
downstairs that she could see. She stepped farther inside, looked around, and saw her large suitcase at the
foot of the bed.

"How do you like it?" Germaine asked.

"It's lovely." She forgot about the muffled voices.
The room was truly beautiful. Gleaming oak parquet
surrounded a large Oriental-looking wool rug in rich
shades of wine, sand, and blue. The canopied bed,
with its many pillows, was covered with eggshell cro-
chet that matched various old-fashioned doilies on the
rest of the antique furniture. Cream lace hung at the
wide, corniced windows. Time had been pushed back
a hundred years in this room, and Anna felt right at
home.

"Will you need any help unpacking?" Germaine
asked.

"Oh, no. I can manage just fine, thank you."

"Supper's at six-thirty."

"I'll be there. And thank you again."

Germaine closed the door, and Anna inhaled the
swirling fragrance of lavender. She felt completely at
peace and pleasantly surprised. La Maison seemed
much more like a home than a boardinghouse. Of
course, the presence of George Thomas would help.
Anna was already missing her niece, Donanne.

The windows beckoned, drawing Anna to the south
wall for a look down into the garden Germaine had
told her about. It was just as lovely as she expected

it to be, the warm southern climate and rich soil providing for an abundance of spring greenery and colorful, exotic flowers. The yard extended all the way to the long garage that was almost completely hidden by trees, vines, and shrubs. The several garage doors faced the alleyway that bisected the block east to west.

She heard the voices again. G.T. and Mitch appeared below on their way toward the alley, talking, laughing, and gesturing as they followed the flagstone path to one end of the garage. When they disappeared behind the structure, Anna turned away. She hadn't expected to feel lonely for her niece and the children at the Casa del Niños day school this soon.

Unpacking took her mind off the mild feeling of isolation. In each carefully lined drawer, she found a fragrant sachet—dried petals, leaves, and spices tied with satin ribbons in sheer pieces of netting. Rich aromas filled the air with each opening and closing, leaving her feeling pampered and special. Germaine Rankin had a special gift for bringing comfort to those around her, Anna decided. No wonder she had a "full house" most of the time.

When everything was either hung in the closet or tucked into drawers, Anna arranged her makeup and toiletries on the dressing table. Reflected in one of the side mirrors she saw a beautiful three-sectioned silk screen she hadn't noticed before and decided it would be perfect for partitioning off the sitting space in the opposite corner. She didn't see the door behind the screen until she'd moved it several inches.

She stopped, staring at the dark wood of the door, and listened. The voices had returned and they were coming from the next room. The unmistakable richness of the baritone belonged to Mitch McCabe, while the high musical sound of a child was obviously emanating from George Thomas. Anna approached and gingerly tried the knob. It was locked. She sighed with relief, backed away, and quietly replaced the screen.

Adjoining rooms, Anna thought to herself as she sat down in one of the overstuffed chairs in the opposite corner. The idea upset her slightly, though she could think of no reason why. It wasn't as if they had to share. But then she didn't sleep in the same room with any of her brothers or her uncles or her father, and they always seemed to manage to interfere in her life. It was benign interference, of course; she understood that very well. She had accepted it as love and protection all her twenty-eight years, but it didn't keep her from feeling cloistered and somewhat overpowered at times.

A light tapping sound brought Anna to her feet in an instant. She acknowledged the presence in the hallway by opening the door, then took a quick step back.

"Germaine thought you might like a little sherry before supper," Mitch said. "You've had a long drive."

Anna's eyes moved from his face to the small wicker tray, to the crystal decanter flanked by two stemmed glasses, then back to the smiling brown eyes. She said nothing.

"I can come back in a few minutes if you're busy," he said.

Anna stared for a second longer, realized how uncomfortable she was making him, and took another step back. "Come in," she said softly.

Mitch strode toward the two chairs in the corner and put the tray down on the small round table between them. "I've always liked this room," he said, as he pulled the heavy crystal stopper from the decanter and began pouring the sherry. He motioned with the hand that held the transparent lid. "That bed belonged to my parents when they first got married back in…" He grinned at her and nodded. "Guess I shouldn't go telling family secrets just yet. That was a long time ago."

Anna relaxed a bit with his easy banter. "I'm glad to know there are other families with secrets," she said.

Mitch replaced the stopper and lowered the decanter to the tray. "Come from a big family, do you?" he asked, glancing back, then picking up the two glasses.

"Not as large as some, but, yes, you could say that. Seven uncles and two aunts on my father's side, four uncles and three aunts on my mother's side, three older brothers and one younger sister.''

''Whoa! That's a houseful,'' he said, holding one glass toward her. When she took it, he touched it with his. ''A toast to large families, then.''

Anna took a sip of the sherry and lowered her glass. ''You're also part of a large family?'' she asked.

He motioned for her to sit down, then sat down himself. ''Not compared to yours,'' he said, leaning forward, resting his elbows on his knees. ''It seems even smaller since we're scattered all over.'' He pointed south. ''Uncle Thomas lives down in the delta country, Aunt Germaine lives here, my parents are still in New Mexico, and my brother and sister are in California and Connecticut, respectively.''

''Oh, my.'' The thought of being separated by such distances gave her pause. ''Do you ever get together?'' she asked.

''We've had a couple of reunions in the last ten years,'' he said, his thoughts making him smile with the memory.

The happy dimpling of his cheeks was particularly pleasing to Anna, and she realized that she wasn't nearly as uncomfortable in his company as she'd expected to be. ''Where did you meet?'' she asked, genuinely interested now.

''St. Louis the first time.'' He shook his head. ''Lousy weather, clouds and wind the whole time, but it was about the halfway point for everybody. We got together here last year." He took a drink of wine. "Your bunch ever get together?"

"Practically every day, in one combination or another," Anna said with a smile. "Most of us live in San Antonio."

"Must be nice," Mitch said thoughtfully.

"Sometimes."

Mitch looked at her. "You don't like having all those relatives around?"

Anna shrugged. "It isn't that, exactly. It's just that you're kind of on call all the time, if you know what I mean."

"Explain."

"With six family-run businesses all in the same town, there are always emergencies to attend to. Whoever happens to be free gets called in to help out. It's an efficient way to handle things, but no one gets much time off."

"So what do you do most of the time?" he asked.

"Cook."

"Oh, yeah. Germaine said you're a chef."

"In my father's restaurant."

"How about that?" Mitch leaned back in the chair. "I've never met a lady chef before."

"There aren't a lot of us around," Anna said.

"Well, I'm pleased to know one of the few. Maybe you can teach me a thing or two in the kitchen. A man can get pretty tired of his own cooking."

"You live alone?" Anna asked, inordinately

pleased, for some reason, to hear that he cooked his own meals.

"Even more alone than alone," he said. "Not a house or a human in sight for as far as you can see in every direction."

"Winkler County," Anna said.

"Dust bowl of the universe…and I love it. Peaceful."

"Sounds divine."

"Feeling all cramped up in the city?" he asked.

"Sometimes I do."

"Know the feeling myself," he said. "By the time this vacation's over, I'll be rarin' to get back out west."

"Then why do you come?"

Mitch flexed the fingers of his left hand one at a time. "Have to keep in practice," he said.

"I don't understand."

"I'll try to make a long story short. An old buddy of mine plays the fiddle in a band down on Bourbon Street. He likes to rest up after Mardi Gras, so I come and sit in for him while he goes out to my place and baby-sits my horses. It's a little more complicated than that—I owe him—but you get the picture."

Anna nodded. "So you play the violin?"

"The fiddle," he corrected. "If you ever heard me play, you'd understand the distinction."

She smiled and shook her head. "You don't have

to be modest. You must have quite a skill if you can take the place of a professional musician."

Mitch drained his glass and put it on the table. "Miss Harte, you flatter me. The main thing I do *well* is put a shoe on a horse."

He seemed to be about to leave, and Anna realized that she didn't want him to. She picked up the decanter, removed the stopper, and poured more sherry into his glass. "I don't know a thing about horses," she said lightly. "I've always wanted to learn."

Mitch lifted the glass and sighed. "Admirable creatures," he said, looking through the pale liquid. "Very accommodating most of the time."

Anna reconsidered her desire for him to stay. "I've never thought of acquiescence as necessarily admirable," she said.

Mitch didn't acknowledge her reproach. "Guess I'm talking more about being agreeable than conforming," he said easily. "There's some stubbornness in every creature, but horses can be reasonable if you give them some time to think."

"That's good to know...if you have to deal with horses."

"I guess we could call this lesson number one, couldn't we?"

"How's that?" Anna asked.

"You said you'd always wanted to learn about horses. Or were you just being polite?"

He'd caught her. The ploy to keep him in the room

had backfired, and now she had nothing to say that seemed appropriate. "I'm interested in horses," seemed safe and not altogether untrue.

"Intellectually speaking," he said.

"Well..." Anna glanced across the room, then back to him. "Hands-on experience at this stage is a bit frightening for a city girl."

"You mean more frightening than working with Pep Gutierrez?"

"What do you mean?"

"Formidable," Mitch said seriously, then smiled. "But it's an act."

"I'm glad you told me."

"All you have to do is exactly what he says. You'll get along just fine."

"Be agreeable, in other words."

"That's all it takes."

"Shouldn't be any trouble." Anna took another sip of her sherry. "I work with some pretty temperamental people."

"Your father?"

"You're very perceptive, Mr. McCabe." A little too perceptive for comfort, she thought.

"Comes from moving around, I suppose," he said.

"The way you were talking, I thought you'd been a west Texan for a long time."

"Eight years," he said.

The sherry was warming her, dissolving barriers. "And before that?" she asked.

Mitch lowered his glass to rest on his belt buckle and looked toward the ceiling. "Well, let's see, now...I was born in New Mexico, lived in Mimbres till I was fifteen, then moved to Santa Rita and worked in the copper mine for a few years." He looked at her and smiled. "Till I had enough money to get out of the hole."

"Literally and figuratively?" Anna said.

"Physically and financially."

"Then what did you do?"

"This gets pretty boring," he warned.

"I'll stop you when I start to nod off," Anna countered.

He smiled. "Fair enough. I traded a hole for a tunnel, mining potash near Carlsbad. Did a little prospecting for gold in my time off. Then I decided there wasn't any future in the pit or the cave. Came to Louisiana and worked for Uncle George in his cane fields. He had a few hundred acres of sugarcane west of here."

"But you didn't like farming either?" Anna asked.

"I didn't know it until I spent some time working with Uncle Thomas in his orange groves down in the delta. That got me itchin' for a change of scene and some real money."

"So you robbed a bank?"

"More dangerous than that. Roughnecking on the oil rigs in the Gulf."

"They *do* make good money," Anna said. "Why did you quit?"

"No horses," he said simply.

"Oh."

"So I saved up and bought myself two hundred acres of west Texas."

"And you and your horses live happily ever after. Your story wasn't boring at all. I like happy endings."

Mitch leaned forward again. "I would have guessed that."

"Why?"

He shrugged. "I don't know. Just something in your eyes, I guess. Kind of expecting the good things, looking for the good times. Optimistic. Maybe a little naive."

Anna sat up a bit straighter. She felt the pronouncement a bit too judgmental coming from a stranger. "Naive?"

"Hold on, now. I meant that as a compliment."

She relaxed a little. She was used to dealing with powerful, straightforward men like her father—but not accustomed to enjoying it. Feeling relaxed with Mitchell McCabe was a puzzlement. "Then I suppose I should take it as one."

"Your eyes are beautiful...expecting the good things," he said again.

Anna shifted uncomfortably in her chair. "Thank you." It was reasonable to be gracious. She made a show of looking at her watch. ''It's almost six-thirty,'' she said.

''I'm not going to keep you another minute,'' he said. ''You must be hungry after your long drive.'' He finished his sherry in one swallow, stood up, and crooked his elbow. ''May I accompany the lady to the table?''

Anna rose and put her hand through the circle of his arm. ''My pleasure, Mr. McCabe.''

''The pleasure's just beginning,'' he said.

TWO

Philippe Allen François Gutierrez was just as large as his name, and it wasn't only his very ample physical presence that seemed to fill the vast kitchen of Lucullan. Pep's voice reached every corner of the white-tiled room, his orders given in staccato, every word precise, clipped, and to the point.

Anna liked him on sight. Within seconds of her arrival, she was being held in a bear hug, crushed against Pep's spotless white coat, then released to arm's length only to be pulled back again for a kiss on each cheek. One sturdy arm around her shoulder, he then propelled her through the maze of equipment to meet each employee individually.

She couldn't help herself. Her attention was more on the food being prepared than on the names that were being pronounced. It would be necessary to listen attentively later on when orders were called out and the names were spoken again. Hot-milk sponge cake, semisweet chocolate ganache, a coffee-scented soufflé pastry, Fettuccine Verdi Capriccio...

"You'll begin with the duck," Pep was saying. "Ramón will take you through the preparation step by step." He leaned down to whisper in her ear. "He's very protective of the ham. Let him do all the dicing."

Anna nodded. "I understand," she said quietly. Working with the men in her own family had given her a second sense about protecting an ego—and self-preservation.

Ramón proved to be a real sweetheart, in spite of Pep's warning, a smile accompanying every step he took. His thin body moved from stockpot to cutting boards to refrigerators seemingly without effort, and all his instructions were clear and much easier to follow than his footsteps. By day's end, Anna was exhausted and had vowed to lengthen her morning walk to build up the stamina she was obviously going to need.

La Maison was a welcome sight; the mammoth, white-framed two-story structure was an inviting haven after the noisy bustle of Lucullan's kitchen. She was used to the frenzy behind the restaurant's elegant dining room setting, but the extra pressure of learning new techniques had taken its toll. She was ready for a long hot bath and a good night's sleep. She was also ready to see Mitch.

The house was uncommonly quiet, however. It was amazing how so many people living in one house managed to stay out of the way of the others. She'd barely seen any of the other women except at dinner. But she'd expected to at least hear the playful sounds of George and his buddy this evening. They'd continued to play in the living room after dinner last night, and she'd enjoyed hearing the happy sounds and being designated as the imprisoned Princess Leah in their Star Wars campaign.

Odd, she thought, as she drew her bathwater, that she would be missing someone she barely knew. And a man, at that. A frown tugged at her brows as she sank into the hot water. She was obviously displacing the feelings she had for the child, and giving Mitchell McCabe more importance than was due.

What a stroke of good fortune it had been that Germaine would have a child just the same age as her niece, Donanne. She wished she could have gone with George Thomas to his preschool this morning and taken part in the learning and the fun. It would be an entire month before she could return to San Antonio and indulge herself, two mornings a week, in the joy of Donanne's world of children.

The yearning for a child of her own seemed even

more pronounced now, here in the quiet retreat she'd found. The idea had been to escape, to give herself time to think without the constant family demands, the headaches of business. But the conflicts refused to be sorted out in a logical manner. Was a woman who wanted a child of her own *less* a woman if she questioned the value of the presence of a man in her life?

The secret was hers alone, though she longed to tell someone of her innermost desire. No one knew the dream, nor did she dare to share the dream with anyone. The idea of being a single parent would tear at the closely woven fabric of the extended family. The whole of the Harte brigade would gather in force to persuade her that she was quite mad for harboring such antipatriarchal thoughts. Until the decision was made, the wish most dear to her heart would have to remain inviolate.

Santino's was packed when Mitch arrived. Already, the patrons were anticipating a long night of music and dancing. Mitch was already questioning his good sense. Four weeks a year for the past seven years he'd been sitting in for his friend and ex-brother-in-law, Joey Costella.

The greetings from the four other musicians had been exuberant, the hugs and the handshakes welcome and exhilarating. But the debt to Joey had been overpaid. This *had* to be the last vacation in New

Orleans for the express purpose of taking Joey's place.

It wasn't that he didn't enjoy playing the fiddle. He did indeed. Every third Saturday night of each month found him at the grange hall, the rousing cadence of the square dance ingrained in every fiber of his being. It was the west at its rowdy best, the bright colors of whirling skirts, the intricate patterns of the dance, the precision of the clattering steps—and the laughter.

He was hearing laughter now as he carefully lifted the old violin from its tattered case. But the sounds he was hearing seemed forced, somehow influenced more by alcoholic spirits than by the pure enjoyment and accomplishment. He was tempted to tell Honcho that his stay this year would have to be cut short, problems at home, a broken oil rig, a pump that had given in to old age.

In a circuitous way, it was the oil that had brought him here in the first place. He'd met Joey on an oil rig in the Gulf of Mexico. Both men had had a wish for the future, though their dreams had been different in the extreme. Joey had always wanted to be a musician; Mitch had always wanted to own horses. Joey's sister, Betina, had been a real estate broker in west Texas, and Joey had brought her and Mitch together.

Mitch and Betina had been married the same day that the contract for the two hundred acres had been signed. Three years later, to the day, Betina had packed up and left. She said she couldn't stand the isolation and wanted to get back to civilization. The real reason had been a three-year battle over the expense of certain of Mitch's decisions. He'd been drilling for oil instead of water. She'd tried to come back a year later when Mitch had hit his first oil well.

But Joey still took the credit for Mitch's good fortune. "Without me, you'd still be uncoupling drill pipe and slogging around in the slime for someone else's profit, good buddy," Joey often reminded him. Mitch wasn't sure all his wealth was worth it, but he was sure that the repayment was at an end. He hadn't known it until he'd met Anna Harte.

Anna. The name felt soft when he said it, no harsh angles, no harsh sounds. The name had been on his tongue and in his mind all night. None of the other women he'd met at supper last evening had given him anything approaching the measure of content Anna had, he thought as he tightened, then rosined, his bow and began to tune his instrument. But as congenial and interested as she'd been earlier, there'd also been a certain distance. When the other women at the dining table had been obviously interested in him, Anna had kept silent, retreating into a place deep within her own being, a private place where no one else was permitted.

It was the only place he wanted to be.

She wasn't sure what had awakened her, but it was just as well since she'd forgotten to set her alarm for half an hour earlier. Perhaps it was foolish to think that walking an extra distance before going to Lucullan would give her more stamina for a long and difficult day. That extra half hour of sleep seemed infinitely preferable to the exercise.

"Get going, lazy bones," she whispered to herself and managed to swing her legs out of bed and sit up.

The bright red of her new jogging suit lifted her spirits, and a splash of cold water braced her for the cool morning air. Quiet, tree-lined streets offered an ever-changing scene in the older neighborhood that surrounded La Maison, and the light fog was a pleasant surprise. Her one-hour walk brought color to her cheeks and a lightness to her step that she hadn't thought possible while lying in her warm bed.

The house was still quiet when she returned, and it was early enough to have a leisurely breakfast before dressing for the day. Germaine's well-equipped kitchen left nothing to be desired either in the way of appliances or selection of food. The coffeemaker chugged into life while a fluffy omelet bubbled in the skillet. How pleasant it must be to cook for one's self, she mused, as she buttered her toast. How pleasant to jostle one omelet instead of ten at a time. Why had Mitch complained? She wondered, as she sat down to her solitary breakfast. The only thing that could have made the experience more pleasant would have been the presence of a child.

"I thought I heard someone roaming around down

here." The voice came from the door straight ahead of her.

Anna looked up to find Mitch leaning casually against the doorframe. He was fully dressed even at this early hour in a pair of tan cords, a white western shirt, and boots, but his hair was pleasingly tousled, as if he wasn't quite ready for the day to begin. "I'm sorry. I didn't mean to disturb you," she said.

Mitch advanced into the room. "You didn't disturb me. I thought I was tired, but I haven't been able to get to sleep for over an hour."

"You're just now going to bed?" she asked, forgetting about his late-night hours at Santino's.

"Musicians keep strange hours." He turned a chair around, straddled it, and sat down. "So, how was your first day in Pep's lair?"

"Interesting…exhausting," she said with a smile. The smile was for the sight of the man sitting across from her. He looked so comfortable and not the least ill at ease.

"But you had a good night's sleep?" he asked, hoping she would tell him that thoughts of him had kept her awake.

"Slept like a rock," she said, then stood. "Let me get you some coffee. Oh…maybe not. It might keep you awake. How about some eggs? Toast? A glass of milk?"

"Coffee," he said, rising, then crossing to the cabinet for a mug. "I don't care much about sleeping anymore."

"I get that way sometimes," Anna said, as he approached her. Then he was before her, towering over her, making her feel very uncomfortable. She poured the coffee and turned away. "I think it's excitement about whatever you've just done. Something like that," she said with her back to him.

Or something you haven't been able to do, Mitch thought to himself. He wanted to reach out and touch her, tell her not to fear him. "Guess you could be right about that," he said finally, turning back to the kitchen table.

"So your night was full of excitement?" Anna asked, as they sat down again. She felt that she had to keep the conversation going.

"I guess we furnished a little. Everybody seemed to have a good time."

"I like the idea that people enjoy my work, don't you?"

Mitch wrapped both his hands around the mug, leaned on the back of the chair he straddled, and smiled. "The horses love my work," he said.

"You lost me. I thought we were talking about playing the fiddle."

"That's not my best thing," Mitch said thoughtfully.

His statement wasn't one she could respond to immediately. Added to that, his presence was so much more disturbing than it had been on her first night here. Perhaps she'd been foolish to invite him into her room, to encourage a friendship before the time was right. She couldn't let the silence continue between them. "I think I understand," she said. "Cooking isn't my best thing either."

"But that's what you do. I thought that's what you liked to do."

"It is." Anna took a sip of coffee. "But I like taking care of children better," she said evenly.

"Then that's what you should do," Mitch said.

"I indulge myself two mornings a week. One of my aunts has a Casa del Niños preschool." Anna couldn't help but smile. "What fun it is."

He leaned closer. "Your eyes light up in the prettiest way when you're happy about something, Anna." He watched as the color, already glowing in her cheeks, brightened even further. "I meant to tell you that last night."

Her cup clattered in the saucer as she put it down. "Are you sure you wouldn't like some breakfast?" she asked. "I'd be glad to fix you something. Really."

Mitch shook his head. "Thanks, but I'm not the least bit hungry right now," he said.

Neither am I, Anna thought, and looked at the half-finished omelet still on her plate. Strange. She'd had a ravenous appetite just a few moments ago.

"Maybe it's too early," he went on. "Or too late,

depending on how you look at it.'' He shrugged. ''Old Blue usually has me up by this time at home.''

''Old Blue?''

''My stud. A hungry horse. Always hungry...for one thing or the other.'' Mitch cleared his throat. ''He calls me out for his first feed around five-thirty every morning.''

Anna gave a little laugh. ''How does he do that?''

''All kinds of strange noises. Mostly it sounds something like grumbling.''

''A hungry male is hard to deal with,'' Anna said.

He thought he'd heard a trace of disgust in her tone. ''You know a lot about males?'' he asked.

''I should. I live with three of them, my father and two brothers.''

Mitch breathed a sigh of relief. The question had been a dangerous one, and he'd regretted asking it the moment it had been spoken. ''Case closed,'' he said.

Anna reached for his mug. ''I'll get you some more coffee,'' she said as she stood up. She needed to put some distance between her and the charming way he had of putting her at her ease as soon as he'd taken her off balance.

Mitch watched her walk away. Her easy movement in the bright red suit brought a secret smile to his lips. Did she know how beautiful she was? He wondered. Could she guess what he'd been thinking about ever since he'd come into the room? Of course she couldn't. That distance was still between them, an invisible cushion of her own making. She was hiding behind it and trusting it to keep her safe.

"You're going to spoil me if you keep waiting on me," he said when she handed him the coffee.

Anna picked up her plate and silverware. "You're objecting to being waited on?" she asked.

"Not objecting, just commenting."

"Most of the men I know expect it," she said on her way to the sink.

"That's interesting."

A firm hand turned the faucet and water splashed across her dish. With an anger she didn't know she felt, she poked the remainder of her breakfast down the garbage disposal and flipped the switch on the wall. When there wasn't a trace left, she turned the machine off and looked at him. "Interesting?"

"Maybe you just don't know the right men."

Anna crossed the stove and picked up the skillet. "Now that's a line I haven't heard before," she said, pointing at him with the heavy pan, then heading back to the sink. "Congratulations."

Mitch shifted in his chair. "Funny. I didn't have you figured as a bitter person."

She sighed and kept her eyes on the job of washing the pan. "I'm not bitter about anything." She turned on the water again and let it run much longer than she needed to. The conversation was getting uncomfortable, and she didn't want to answer any more questions. There were enough questions going unanswered in her own mind already. She pulled a towel from a rack, dried the skillet as she recrossed the room, then put it away with a loud clatter. "I didn't mean to do that," she said.

"Do what?"

"Make so much noise."

"I've upset you."

"No, you haven't."

"Then why are you flitting around the kitchen like a bride preparing her first dinner?"

"Flitting like a bride? What would you know about brides?"

"I had one once."

Anna started another trip to the sink. She didn't want to hear another word about this exasperating man.

Mitch stood up, moved across the room, and stopped her in mid-flight. "I think you're trying to run away from me," he said softly.

She looked at the hand that held her arm, then up into serious eyes. "Why should I be running away from you? I wasn't even aware that you were chasing me."

"I know. It's that innocence I was talking about. A very intriguing complication to an enchanting personality."

"I don't want to hear this again."

"You said you'd take it as a compliment before."

Anna started to pull away.

"Wait. Don't run away again. Let's call a truce."

"Doesn't there have to be some conflict before a truce can be declared?"

Mitch released her arm. "Don't you feel it?"

"I don't feel anything," Anna said flatly, knowing all the time it was a lie. At this very moment she was experiencing a most delightful nervousness and a very unfamiliar fear.

His hands balled into fists, then relaxed. "I was afraid of that," he said, disappointed for a moment. But she hadn't walked away when he'd let her go. There was still a bit of hope. "We have a month here together. What say we give it a try?"

"Give *what* a try? Being civil? Being friendly? Something more than that, perhaps?"

"All of the above," Mitch said.

"This may come as a surprise, but I'm a very old-fashioned type of person."

"Meaning?"

"'Something more' is out of the question."

"You were being sarcastic, then?" he asked.

"I don't know any other way to handle advances like that."

"You could just say no when the time came," he suggested.

"By that time it might be too late," she countered.

Mitch nodded. "I see."

"What do you see?"

He reached for her hand, held it gently, but kept

the same distance between them. "I see that you're
not a stranger to passion...that you know what's going on and have the strength to make your own rules
and stick to them. I admire that."

Anna was taken aback by his insight and his truth-
fulness. She forgot about her first instinct to pull her
hand away from his. The act of holding hands was
becoming more pleasurable by the second. Denying
it wouldn't make the sunshine go away. "You're a
very persuasive man," she said finally. "But you
could have chosen a much easier target."

"I wasn't looking for a target," he said quietly.

"Remind me to ask what you *were* looking
for..."—she glanced at the clock that sat on the top
of the refrigerator—"...when I have the time to listen
carefully to your answer." Mitch lifted her hand to
his lips. The kiss was brief, but thoughtfully tender.
Until this moment she would have thought he was the
type of man who would try to sweep a woman off
her feet with a forceful embrace.

"Thank you," he said, then lowered her hand and
held it in both of his.

"For what?"

"For promising me more of your time."

"Did I make a promise?" she asked.

"I'm not going to pressure you into it, if that's
what you mean."

Anna took a step back but kept her hand in his.
"You're a nice man, Mitchell McCabe." On second

thought, she stepped forward and gave him a soft kiss on the cheek, then backed away again.

For an insane moment he wanted to wrap her in his arms and hold her close. Too soon, he warned himself in time. Maybe they would never be more than friends, but that's how it had to begin. Just wanting much more would not make it come true. He leaned forward and returned a kiss on the cheek.

"Ugh! Kissing!"

Both Anna and Mitch turned to look toward the door. George Thomas stood in footed pajamas, brandishing his long plastic "laser stick." "Princess Leah doesn't love Darth Vader." George dropped his weapon and ran toward them.

Mitch lifted him into his arms and kissed his cheek. "Is it okay for Darth Vader to kiss Luke Skywalker?"

George made a show of wiping the kiss away and wrinkled his nose in mock disgust. When he stopped wiggling, he looked at Mitch. "I'm hungry," he said seriously.

Anna smiled. "Germaine was right."

"I've never seen him when he wasn't hungry," Mitch said. "How about some eggs, partner?"

George drew back with a frown on his face. "Is that all you can cook?" he asked.

Mitch patted him playfully on the stomach. "I can make toast."

The boy cocked his head from side to side while he thought the offer over. "Cinnamon toast?"

Mitch shrugged at Anna, then looked back at George. "You help me, and I'll give it a try, okay?"

George pointed at Anna. "She can do it," he said knowingly.

"*She,* my friend, has to get dressed for work. You're stuck with me."

George squirmed and Mitch put him down on the floor. "Okay," George said without further comment.

"That was easy," Mitch said to Anna, a surprised look on his face.

"That's one of the things I love about children. They can be reasonable if you give them the facts."

"Why do I feel like I've just been reprimanded?" Mitch said, smiling.

"Guilty conscience?"

"Aren't you late for work?"

"No." Anna gave a short laugh. "But I'm going, I'm going. The kitchen's yours."

"Thanks," he said dubiously.

"You're welcome."

Into your life? he wanted to ask. "See you later," he said instead.

He waited until she'd left the room. "You go wash up for breakfast, young man," he told George.

When the boy had run out, Mitch sat down at the table and lowered his head to crossed arms. He was suddenly very tired. He was also feeling very lonely; he had to admit it. It hadn't occurred to him to feel this way since his days on the oil rigs, days when time "on" was matched with time off, and he'd spent seemingly endless hours with his mates playing cards in the small, sterile quarters furnished by the company.

What was it about Anna Harte that had him so intrigued? he wondered. Of course she was pretty—beautiful, in fact. He loved the way she looked, the way her hazel eyes shone when she talked about children, the way her lips parted slightly when she was thinking, the way her dark, lustrous hair moved when she nodded her head. Every curve, every soft and rounded contour, he could see, even when she wasn't there. Everything about her was stamped indelibly on his memory.

Just one thing eluded him. How was she different from the other women who'd come into his life? There was a mystery about her. One might even call it an aloofness, some special reserve. She had a way of looking at him, a certain twinkle in her eye, as if she were guarding a secret with that little bit of a smile, a secret that no one else could know.

What was it she'd said when he'd offered to carry her suitcase upstairs? "I can handle it." That was it. Well, that was part of it, anyway. She didn't seem to need him—or anyone. No, it was different from that. She didn't seem to need a man.

"Don't cry, Mitchell."

A small hand was patting him on the back. Mitch quickly lifted his head. "Hey, partner. I was just catchin' forty winks. Up all night, you know," he said as he stood.

George grabbed his hand and walked beside him to the refrigerator. "Did ja play 'Ragtime Band'?"

"Sure did."

"I'm playin' the trumpet next year."

"Is that a fact?" Mitch said as he reached for the butter and the bread.

"They're small." George held up both hands to measure the length.

"So how'd you come to choose a trumpet, old man?"

"It's the only thing they have," George said simply. "Nobody gets to choose in the first grade."

"Oh."

"Have to wait till I'm *your* big before I can do anything I want to."

It's even tougher then, partner, he thought. So very, very much tougher.

Three

Cinnamon toast. Cinnamon toast. The more often she repeated it in her mind, the sillier the words began to sound. There wasn't one person in her family who didn't know how to make cinnamon toast. What a strange and tiny world she'd lived in for all these years, she thought, as warm water poured over her from the showerhead. How very sheltered she'd always been—with an overprotective mother, a strict patriarch for a father, and three big brothers always to take her side even when she was in the wrong.

Home had usually seemed the perfect place to be. At least it had until her younger sister, Charleen, had begun having husband troubles. That was when the questions had started, when the doubts had squirmed their way into her peaceful existence.

I'm not going to think about this anymore today, Anna told herself as she toweled off and began drying her hair. But as she lifted the strands with the rounded brush and the warm air lulled her, she couldn't help but think about Charleen. Beautiful Charleen, the lovely girl who believed in the ideal marriage—until the fantasy became a nightmare. But the child was not an illusion.

Donanne, the child of that fantasy marriage, would be better off without the father who complained constantly if things weren't just so, the father who wasn't content unless everything went according to his own plan. That's what Anna had told her sister. That's what Anna sincerely believed. She had even come to think of herself as the maiden aunt—the objective outsider—when it came to family problems, but a woman who could take the children into her life and into her heart. If there was a right man for Charleen, it certainly was not Jerry Hayford or any of the men Anna knew.

A "right" man?

Anna tried to imagine Mitch's face reflected in the mirror beside hers. He was shaving. No, he was just smiling. She moved a step to the right. He wasn't there at all, had no business there. She moved another step to the right and could no longer see herself. That's where her mother would be if her father wanted to use the mirror, off to the side, out of his way. Waiting, she was always waiting on one thing or another, instructions, orders, her turn.

If her mother's "turn" never came, Stephanie didn't complain. Vincent ruled, no question about that, and his subjects dared not to ask any questions. He was a good father, a good husband, strict but indulgent—as long as he was in command.

Anna put her hair drier away, slipped into fresh underwear and a long, velour terry robe, then went back into her bedroom. There would be plenty of time for analyzing later. She'd almost finished with her makeup when she heard a tap on the door.

"Just a minute." She touched the lipstick to her bottom lip one more time, then went to the door and opened it. There was no one there. She went back to the dressing table, sat down, and the tapping repeated.

Anna turned and looked around the room. Could there be a ghost in residence? She wondered. The house was old and probably had an interesting history. The idea of a ghost pleased her, but with so many people living here there was surely a logical explanation for the knocking.

"Whatever you're selling, we don't want any," she said aloud, then smiled. It was an old custom of her father's, a joke of sorts from school days when the telephone and the doorbell were constantly ringing, her father's way of startling young suitors and girlfriends.

"I just wanted to apologize for disturbing your breakfast," a voice said from across the room.

Anna was puzzled, but she recognized the voice. It had to be coming from the other side of the door that joined Mitch's room to hers. She didn't know whether to be gracious and accept his apology, or to be angry that he was disturbing her in the privacy of her room. A neutral response seemed even more appropriate than either of the others.

"Shouldn't you be getting some sleep?" she asked, picking up her brush and continuing her preparations to dress.

"I'm headed for the bed right now. But I didn't want you to leave without knowing that I didn't mean to upset you this morning."

"You didn't upset me."

"Not even a little?" he asked.

"I'm not as fragile as you might think," Anna said, as she crossed to the closet. Unbelievably, she was enjoying their long-distance conversation. Her hand stopped and rested on a blue jumper. She was anticipating an answer, but she heard only silence. Tugging the dress and a cream white blouse off their hangers, she turned toward the door.

"Are you asleep on your feet?" she asked.

"Not quite. It just takes a few days to get used to the new hours."

"You should have taken me up on my offer for breakfast," she said, pulling on the blouse.

"You're probably right." *But I couldn't have eaten a thing,* he thought. In Anna's presence, food had to be the furthest thing from his mind.

"I hope the coffee doesn't keep you awake," Anna said, as she stepped into the royal blue knit. "I make it pretty strong."

"You don't have to worry about the coffee. I don't think anything could keep me awake now."

"I'm glad to hear it."

"I'm glad I got to talk to you before you left."

"Have a good sleep," Anna said, reaching into the closet again for her coat.

"Enjoy your day."

Anna paused before the door to the hallway. Why was she hesitating to leave? she wondered, the knob still stationary in her hand. "See you later," she said, fusing the contact again with her voice. There was no answer, and Anna experienced a brief twinge of disappointment. She shrugged it off, then left the room.

But the feeling wouldn't leave her. All the way to Lucullan she could not get Mitchell McCabe out of her mind. She couldn't step aside and cover the fictional mirror image; his face appeared in her thoughts and wouldn't go away. Even more persistent than his image was the touch of his hand, the feel of his lips on the curve of her cheek. She wondered what had possessed her to make the first move, to kiss him first.

She'd never been so bold before. Well, the kiss had only been a tiny peck, she told herself. It had been pleasurable, but it wouldn't happen again. She couldn't let it happen again.

A glance at her watch when she stopped in the parking lot assured her that she was early. That's the way she liked to be, early and eager. It was the best way to get along in the world of schedules and time pressures. Her hand gripped the door handle, then stopped in its downward motion. All the schedules she found herself adapting to were those made up by men.

She harbored no real resentment. What she felt was more closely akin to simple discomfort, a need to pursue a life of her own. But no matter how hard she tried to imagine an acceptable existence, one that began with a husband, perhaps a house, respectable mortgage payments, she could not. The one and only thing she knew for certain was that she wanted a child. She had so much love to give.

Get your mind back on cooking, she told herself, and opened the door. At some point a special man would have to come into her life. He would have to be someone who could understand how she felt, someone who would give her what she wanted in exchange for a few pleasant moments, then be more than willing to move on and out of her life.

Had he really said that nothing could keep him awake? Still fully clothed, Mitch lay pondering his brief conversation through the door a long time after

Anna had left for work. He supposed he could try counting horses again, but it seemed a futile gesture. All he could see was Anna's beautiful face and voluptuous body as he tossed restlessly on top of the covers. The violin case caught his attention as he turned on his side again. It gave him an idea.

Germaine had exactly what he needed in her desk in the kitchen, and he went back upstairs with a pen and a pad of stick-on papers in the pocket of his shirt. Several minutes later he'd posted a note on Anna's door.

Dear Anna,
Would like to exchange a night at Santino's for a cooking lesson. Will tell you details in the morning.

Mitch

He pressed the note onto her door at eye level, gave it a pat for good luck, then walked the length of the hall and knocked on Carolyn's door. After a brief conversation with Germaine's oldest tenant, he went back to his room. This time he decided to undress and get comfortable.

The French Quarter was at its riotous best three nights later. Carolyn had warned Anna to be prepared for a wild time, but the multitude of sensory delights was still a surprise. The two women had followed a

street band from the parking lot, been sidetracked by
a troupe of jugglers on a second street corner, then
delayed once again by a group of performing acro-
bats. Delectable aromas surrounded them on all sides,
everything from the authentic Lebanese Hagi Baba-
Burger to the essence of roast prime rib, lobster with
garlic butter, and exotic Szechuan delights.

Anna had almost declined Mitch's invitation, but
now she was glad that she hadn't. Though the atmosphere was much like the Paseo del Río in San Antonio, there was a distinctively different flavor to New
Orleans festivities. The visitors here in the French
Quarter seemed to concentrate more fully on leaving
their inhibitions at home. It was *almost* like being at
home, but without the restraints.

Not only was the atmosphere different, but the arrangements for her date, if it could be called that, had
been unusual in the extreme. There was to be no calling at the door at the specified time, no formality of
planning as there had always been in her father's
home. Anna was to ride with one of the other women
from La Maison, leaving the house sometime around
ten o'clock at night. She and Carolyn would then
meet Carolyn's boyfriend on Chartres Street at the
Blue Orange Gift Shop, which Randy owned. They
were to dine, just the three of them, at The Vieux
Carré. If all went well, they were to arrive at Santino's
in time for the last show.

Santino's proved to be one of the more lively nightspots in the French Quarter. The three of them had been in several other clubs before arriving, so Anna had grounds to compare. The effect was completely western, pointing out once again Germaine's reference to New Orleans' exotic blend of customs and cultures. She was learning that a similar meld took place in the Creole cooking, and that New Orleans meant "round the clock" eating.

Even at a quarter to one in the morning, Santino's had a full house, but a quick check with the man at the door assured them that a front table had been reserved. The only music to be heard when they arrived came from a corner jukebox, and Anna was mildly disappointed that she couldn't see Mitch right away. She was tempted to go wandering. A dark red curtain hung over the doorway at one side of the stage, and she was sure she would find him if she went behind it.

Not that Carolyn and her date, Randy, were poor company. They'd been expert guides and shown her a wonderful time. The food at The Vieux Carré had been outstanding, the pampano *en papillote* a pure delight and a dish she intended to introduce at Celebración del Río as soon as she got home. The entertainment at Crazy Shirley's and The New Blue Angel had been excellent. Anna had no complaints, but she wasn't in the habit of going out at all. Aunt Anna usually did the baby-sitting.

Somehow she felt that she would have been more

comfortable if Mitch had been with them. During
these first few days of her stay, they'd become closer
in an easy, casual sort of way. She was used to his
early morning return now; she'd even come to expect
the sound of his car in the alleyway to wake her up
in plenty of time for her long walk.

Breakfast had changed, too. Not much, but in ad-
dition to cooking for herself she was now heating
milk in a small pan so that he could have the *café au
lait* that he liked in the mornings. His company was
welcome now, also. There were no more remarks
about flitting around the kitchen or being upset. He
was true to his word; he demanded no more than she
was willing to give. She was actually starting to look
forward to their brief morning time together.

The crowd behind her hushed its collective voice,
and Anna automatically looked toward the doorway
beside the small stage. The first man to come through
the curtain had to be the man Mitch had described as
Honcho, the leader of the group. He was no more than
five-foot-five in high-heeled cowboy boots, and he
sported the most luxurious black beard Anna had ever
seen. The applause began and continued until all five
men had climbed the two steps to the stage and taken
their instruments in hand. Then everyone in the congenial gathering became silent.

Anna couldn't take her eyes off Mitchell McCabe.
The violin added a new dimension to the tough western "bronco." She had no word for it, but his interest

in music seemed to round and soften a rough-edged image. He played with a skill she didn't expect and a vitality that perfectly matched the jubilant spirit in the club. She might have thought that playing the fiddle would detract from the purely masculine aura that surrounded him, but the effect was exactly the opposite. The women in the audience around her obviously thought so, too, and the unrestrained spirit of the French Quarter invaded her reserve.

She clapped in delight, flirted with him openly, and sang along when the audience did whether she knew the words or not. Without the least embarrassment, she stood up and smiled at those around her when Mitch announced that he wanted everyone to meet his friend, Anna. She felt proud to know him, proud to be acknowledged as a friend. It was close to a feeling she'd had before, when Donanne had told the children in the preschool that Anna was her favorite aunt.

When Honcho announced that The Pecos Tide was about to play its last number, Anna was disappointed and wished she had been able to come earlier. But nervousness soon shadowed the sense of loss. She had no idea what a date with Mitch would be like; she had no idea what might be expected. Most places in the French Quarter closed by two in the morning, but he'd made a point to reserve the night.

People began leaving as soon as the band had gone backstage. Carolyn and Randy sat with her until Mitch returned to the table, then left after hellos and goodbyes had been said. Mitch hesitated only a moment before taking her hand.

"So, what did you think of Bourbon Street?"

"I thought you were terrific."

"That wasn't the question," he said, teasing, but obviously pleased with the answer.

"I've had a very nice evening," she said.

"Hmm, very nice. Sounds…very nice." He cocked his head to one side and smiled. "Shall we see if we can make that a *sensational* evening?"

"It really has been, Mitch…and I did mean it. You were terrific."

"Come on," he said, pulling her up beside him. "Let's get out of here before they lock us in." He hugged her close. "On second thought, that wouldn't be so bad."

"Mitch?"

"Okay, okay. Just a slip of the halo."

Mitch knew the French Quarter well, and after locking his fiddle in the trunk of his car, they were soon entering an all-night coffee shop. On the way to the table, he spoke briefly to the waiter, and shortly after they were seated there were two steaming cups of chicory-laced *café au lait* and a basket of fresh, hot French doughnuts.

"The best I've ever tasted," Anna said after she'd tried one of the sugary *beignets*.

"Coming from you, that's quite a compliment," Mitch said.

Anna smiled. "I feel as if I've been eating continuously all evening."

"You're not worrying about your weight, are you?" Mitch asked, eyeing her appreciatively.

"Not yet, but I do have to watch my sampling."

"Hazards of the workplace?" he asked.

"In the extreme," Anna said.

"I'm happy to announce that you've done a commendable job."

"Thank you. I could say the same for you."

He took a bite and chewed it with a satisfied expression on his face. "I don't have any problem with sampling. If you could taste my cooking, you'd know what I mean."

"I guess I owe you a lesson now," Anna said.

"Just don't make it too tough on me. My skills in the kitchen are limited, at best."

"I don't believe that for a minute."

"Why do you say that?"

"After tonight, I'm convinced that you're a man of many talents. You just haven't had enough experience."

Mitch grinned at her. "Will you remedy that?"

Anna looked at him over her cup. "Are we talking about the same thing?" she asked.

"I sincerely hope so."

"Is your halo slipping again?"

"With you, it's hard to keep it in place."

"Mitch…"

"That makes you uncomfortable, doesn't it?" he asked seriously.

"Yes."

"Can you tell me why?" he asked.

Anna lowered her cup and looked at him. She'd never told anyone her most cherished secrets. "I don't know why you'd want me to," she said.

Mitch reached across the small table and took her hands. "Because I care about you very much, Anna Harte."

"How can that be? We haven't known each other that long."

"How long is it supposed to take?"

Anna shook her head and looked down. "I don't know."

"So I'm not the only one here who lacks experience," he said calmly.

She looked at him. "I'm sure you've had infinitely more experience *outside* the kitchen," she said.

"Then we can share...trade secrets. Just imagine how bright we'll both be when school's out."

"You make it sound very simple."

"Friendship should be simple."

"Are you sure that's what you want?" Anna asked.

"More than anything else," he said.

Her hands pulled away from his as she leaned back in her chair. "I do feel very close to you," she said softly. Maybe it was time to share her idea with someone who could be objective. If what he wanted "more than anything else" was friendship, perhaps he was the perfect person to talk to. She leaned forward.

"Have you ever wanted something so badly that you have a hard time thinking about anything else?" she asked.

He could barely keep from telling her that he felt that way right now, but the fear of losing her trust kept him from it. "Yes," he answered simply.

"There's something I want very much..." Tears threatened, and she had to pause a moment before she could go on. She'd known it would be difficult; that was why she'd never spoken of her dream to anyone. But now the temptation to share it seemed overwhelming.

"A child," she whispered.

"A child?"

Her head bowed, then rose and bowed again in affirmation.

Mitch had never felt more confused in all his life. He had no idea what she was telling him. Was she married? Was her husband sterile? Was she herself incapable of conceiving? Had she lost a child before birth? Had she lost a child to an accident or some disease? *Please don't let me hurt her,* he prayed.

"I'm not sure I understand what you're saying, Anna," he said softly. Large, innocent eyes looked up at him. "Will you tell me what you mean?" he asked.

Anna took a slow, steadying breath and let it out. "I want a child of my own," she said.

Mitch frowned. "And your husband doesn't. Is that it?"

"I don't have a husband."

"I see." He didn't really see at all, but he was relieved to hear that she wasn't married. He rubbed thoughtfully at his chin while looking at her coffee cup. Then his hand turned palm up in a helpless gesture. "Your fiancé wants to get married, but he doesn't want to have children. Right?"

"I don't have a fiancé, either."

"Oh." He could feel his jaws tightening with frustration. Why was she refusing to be specific? he wondered. Then he concluded that what she had to say must be a very painful revelation.

"Did you...have a...a child once?" he asked haltingly.

Anna shook her head.

"But you have...or you had a husband."

"No."

The truth invaded all at once. "You want a child, but you have no husband and no fianceé."

Anna looked away from him, across the room. Every engagement ring and every wedding band caught her eye. "That's right," she said finally.

"I think I understand," he said cautiously.

"You're not offended?" she asked.

Mitch rubbed at his forehead and sighed. "Should I be?" he asked.

"I wouldn't have been surprised if you had been."

He gazed at her steadily. "Then maybe I *don't* understand," he said.

There was no careful choice of words that would explain. She'd gone too far. It was time to be blunt. "I want a child, but I don't want a husband."

"Ah..." Mitch nodded as if he understood, but he was more confused than ever. She could simply be sharing her innermost dreams, or she could be trying to include him in the conspiracy. She could be using him as a sounding board, seeking his opinion, or she could be asking—

"You...uh...have a plan, do you?" he asked.

Anna shook her head. "No. No plan."

He sighed. "So this is just kind of like a wish?"

She gathered her courage. He'd taken it much better than she thought anybody would. "I'd say it's much more than a wish."

"You've given this a lot of thought?"

"A lot," she assured him.

"Then you won't mind if I ask," he said, the tension mounting throughout his body.

"Ask what?"

He kept his voice to a whisper. "How in blazes are you going to do it?"

"That's the problem," she said quietly.

"The only one?" he asked, astounded by her naiveté. If he didn't know for certain that she was dead serious, he would have felt like laughing.

Anna shrugged. "My parents may be a little upset."

Mitch looked at her in disbelief. "You haven't told them about this...this dream of yours?"

"Just you," she said. "You're the only one who knows."

He felt as if his world had been turned upside down, and he wanted to shout "Why me?" In all his thirty-six years he'd never been confronted with anything that had thrown him off balance the way this had. With fists balled as tightly as watch springs, he took another look at those beautiful, innocent eyes— and he suddenly felt very privileged.

"You honor me, Anna Harte."

Four

"Thank goodness! I thought you two might be here," Carolyn said as she approached their table and sank into a chair. Randy remained standing behind her. "I'm really sorry about disturbing you like this, but we've got a slight problem."

Mitch couldn't believe that Carolyn had been able to pick the absolutely worst time to interrupt their conversation. The muscles in his neck tightened, and he could feel his temper bristling beneath a controlled calm. But she couldn't possibly have known, he realized in time to hold his tongue.

"Are you all right? What is it?" Anna asked, a worried look on her face.

"We're fine. Just a little old car problem again. Randy loaned his out, and mine won't start."

"I can take a look at it," Mitch offered in a steady voice. He was tempted to go to the phone and call them a taxi, but he knew Carolyn needed her car for work.

"Oh, would you? I know you keep those big old oil wells going," Carolyn cooed.

"We'd sure appreciate it, Mitch." Randy held out his hands and turned them over, then back again. "I don't know the back of my hand from the front," he said, grinning.

Carolyn grabbed one of Randy's hands and gave it a squeeze. "He does so many other things *very* well." She looked up at him and smiled. "Don't you, darlin'?"

"Well…" Mitch rose slowly and laid some bills on the table. "Let's go have a look."

"You're a real blessing, Mitchell McCabe," Carolyn said.

"That remains to be seen," Mitch said, looking straight at Anna.

"I hope it's nothing serious," Anna said, turning to Carolyn, avoiding Mitch's eyes. But she couldn't avoid his touch, nor did she want to. While Carolyn described the problem, Mitch and Anna walked arm in arm the few blocks to where the car was parked.

Anna helped him as much as she could, holding the flashlight, moving the beam as Mitch pressed first one thing, then jiggled another. After a few moments he stood back, hands on his hips, and stared at the engine. "I don't see anything wrong under here," he said, then held up a finger. "Let me check one more thing."

After closing the hood, he crouched beside the driver's door, then eased to the ground. In a moment his upper body was under the car. "Now hand me the flashlight," he called out.

Anna did as she was told.

"Anybody got a safety pin?"

Carolyn and Anna looked at one another, shrugged, then began rummaging through their purses in the circle of illumination from the streetlight. Anna came up with the prize, knelt beside the pair of long legs that stuck out from under the car, and handed Mitch the pin. "Will this do?"

"Perfect. Now somebody put the gear in drive."

After uttering one mild oath, and two rattles later, Mitch eased his way out. He stood and dusted off the back of his pants. "Good as new," he said.

"With a safety pin?" Anna asked.

Carolyn and Randy came closer as Mitch explained. "See, there's this little cotter pin that holds the gear-shift mechanism together. Sort of like this." He hooked two fingers together. "The cotter pin broke, and it stayed in drive when you put it in park. I just pulled the two little holes back in line and fastened them with the safety pin."

"And it'll work that way?" Carolyn asked.

"Should last you a good long time," Mitch said.

"Well, I never," Carolyn said.

"Thanks, pal," Randy said, grabbing Mitch's hand and giving it a good shake.

Carolyn rubbed her arms. "It's getting right chilly for a spring night. Anna, you want to ride on home with us? It'll be a cool walk back to Santino's."

"We'll walk," Mitch said quickly, then wrapped his arm protectively around Anna's shoulders.

"We could drop you off," Randy offered.

"We'll walk," Mitch said again.

The muscles in Anna's shoulders tensed in resistance to his authoritarian manner, but she kept silent. She didn't much feel like being with Randy and Carolyn either.

They waited until Carolyn and Randy had tried the ignition. The car started without any trouble. "You're a genius, cowboy," Carolyn said out the window. "Thanks again."

"You two have a good time," Mitch said with a wave, then backed away from the car.

Anna shivered as the car pulled away.

"Are you okay?" Mitch asked, then looked at her. "Did you want to ride with them?"

"It's a little late to ask that, isn't it?"

He wrapped both his arms around her and rubbed warm hands over her back. "Anna, I'm sorry. I was being selfish, wasn't I?"

"Selfish?"

"I wanted to be alone with you," he said softly.

"Shall we go, then?"

Mitch gave her a final hug, left his arm around her waist, and started walking. He could feel her resistance, though it wasn't in any way physical. He'd offended her somehow and he wasn't sure what he'd done wrong. It could be any number of things that had upset her: anxiety and apprehension about telling him of her dream; Carolyn's interruption; his inconsideration in not asking her opinion.

"I've upset you again, haven't I?" he said, as they walked.

"I'm not upset," she said.

"I don't believe you."

"I didn't ask you to believe me."

He stopped and turned to her. "I want to know what's bothering you. I don't like feeling responsible and not knowing what I can do to fix it."

"There's nothing you can do," she said.

"Why don't you let me be the judge of that?"

Anna angled her body away from him and began walking again. "All right, but you may not like what you hear."

"I'll take my chances," he said, matching her steps.

"I resented your authoritarian manner. I'm tired of being treated as if I were something less than a sovereign human being."

"I take it I'm not the first man who's treated you like that?"

"You 'take it' right on that account."

"Your father?"

"I forgive him. He loves me and wants to protect me."

"Then who is this man?"

"Who are *they*, you mean."

Mitch understood. He stopped beside the car door on the passenger's side, unlocked it, then faced her. "You're right," he said. "I don't like what I hear."

"I didn't think you would." Anna reached past him for the handle of the door. "But you don't need to concern yourself. The problem is mine. I allow it to happen."

Mitch stepped back and let Anna open the door for herself. On certain levels she was fighting back against what she considered to be an unprovoked attack on her independence, he thought, as he started around the car. She'd wanted to carry her own suitcase, she opened doors for herself; in many little ways she asserted her right to make decisions for herself. But what about the larger context? The thought struck him like a kick from Old Blue—the baby would be her ticket to self-rule and an opportunity to get out of a family home dominated by men.

His door slammed shut with more force than he'd planned. It might appear that he was angry, but he wasn't. He was frightened. The woman he'd fallen in love with couldn't love him back. Everything he'd prided himself on—forcefulness, shrewd business acumen, cool rationality, and, yes, protectiveness—would be devalued in her eyes.

The drive to La Maison was accomplished in silence. Anna felt she'd said too much already, and Mitch had no idea what he should say or do next. He didn't dare touch her as they walked from the garage to the back door, but when she started up the staircase inside, he could stand the barriers between them no longer. He caught her hand and stopped her.

"We've got to talk," he said.

"Look, Mitch, I'm sorry I bothered you with any of this."

"Bothered me? What in hell are you talking about?"

"Just think of it as being my turn to upset you. I didn't mean to do it, but I did, and now we're both sorry. Let's just drop it, okay?"

"Not on a bet," he said. "You trusted me, and not anyone else—not ever. That has to account for something, doesn't it?"

How right he was about that, she thought, as she searched her mind for an answer. She'd never felt this way about any man, and the mixture of caring and respect and comfort was making her begin to doubt the impossibility of love. Her tidy little world was in turmoil, and she hadn't taken the time to sort through the contradictions. Anna shook her head, turned, and took another step.

Mitch was beside her in a fraction of a second. "You're never going to have a baby if you keep running away from men," he said bluntly.

She felt as if she'd been attacked. "Don't tell me you're not aware of alternative methods," she said, glaring at him.

He knew. "Artificial insemination? You wouldn't do that," he said forcefully.

"What makes you think I wouldn't?" she said, turning away from him.

"Look me straight in the eye and tell me that you would," he said.

Her eyes sought the safety of the floor. There was no way she could bring herself to look at him and say it. Even with her eyes averted she was unable to speak. The possibility of artificial insemination had been discarded over a year ago, her reasons well thought out and logical. She felt she had to know her child's father, otherwise, there would be too many unknowns, too many dangers of all kinds. Also, when the time came, she would have to tell the child about his beginnings in the cold and sterile world of test tubes and Petri dishes and—

Anna straightened and looked at him. "No. I don't want to do that," she said. A tear slipped down her cheek.

Mitch put his arms around her and held her close.

"My Anna," he whispered. "You are so lovely." He kept his arms tightly about her until he felt her take a deep and relaxing breath. "Will you talk with me, Anna?" he asked, all his anger drained away.

Her eyes shone with tears when she looked up at him. There'd been no insistence in his voice. She nodded, clutched her purse in a trembling hand, and walked beside him down the few stairs and into Germaine's cozy parlor.

"I'm going to make a fire," he said, as she sat down. He pulled an afghan from the back of the love seat and covered her, then knelt by the fireplace. His hands worked automatically, pulling kindling from a basket on the hearth, lifting a log from a small stack at the other end, but his mind was on other things. If Anna was going to become a mother, he was going to have to make sure she stayed healthy.

He stared at the tiny flame he'd set and realized that he was doing it again—making decisions for her, thinking of her as someone who needed to be watched over and guided. Had he always been so pompous, so autocratic? he wondered. The light flared as the kindling caught fire, and he stepped back from the warmth.

"That should be going in no time," he said, turning to her. "Are you warm enough?"

"I'm fine, thank you."

"Would you like some brandy?"

She shook her head.

"A glass of water?"

"You don't owe me anything, Mitch."

"I wasn't trying to—"

"Please don't patronize me," she said softly, and he sat down.

Aged wood crackled in the silence of the room, and the fire rose and filled the small stone enclosure, sending its heat into the air. The fragrance of cedar and the old-fashioned comfort of the parlor surrounded them. It was the perfect setting for an intimate conversation, but Mitch hadn't the vaguest idea of how to begin. Confusion still clouded his mind, while the presence of Anna filled his senses with joyful dreams.

"You look so beautiful in the firelight," he said finally. "I love the clothes you wear." He touched the high, lacy collar of the blouse she wore under a soft, coral angora sweater.

She smiled. "You're being very sweet, Mitch. I'm afraid I've been unfair with you tonight."

"Why do you say that?"

"I shouldn't have burdened you. I had no right—"

"Don't say that," Mitch interrupted. "I want to hear anything you want to tell me."

"There's hardly anything more to tell," she said.

"I'm still curious about one thing," he said.

"What?"

He braced himself for a tirade. "Why do you want to have a baby?"

Anna's eyes widened in disbelief. What a crazy

question to ask! And he'd thought that *she* was the naive one! "Because I love children," she said.

He couldn't dispute it. Over the past few days he'd watched her with George Thomas. When they were together, it was as if she lived only for him. She was like a fairy-tale godmother, indulgent but protective, tolerant but not too lenient, generous with her time and her praise and her love. At first he'd thought she might be being polite, catering to him because he was her landlady's child. But there were no flaws in her performance; it wasn't an act.

"You know a lot about children, do you?" he asked.

"Quite a bit," she said.

"About babies, too?"

"And preschoolers, and teens."

"I guess coming from a large family—"

"Don't forget Casa del Niños, too," she reminded him.

He nodded. "Two mornings a week. I remember," he said, then watched her eyes light up.

"You should see those beautiful babies. I can't tell you how much pleasure they give me. There's this little boy, Jamie. He's just learning to pull himself up in the crib where he takes his nap. He gets his little feet under him and goes hand over hand right up a post. It's amazing."

Mitch had never seen anyone rejoice in such a lovely way. He felt as if he'd burst with pride in her unselfish indulgence in pure love. "Tell me some more," he said.

"May I show you?" Anna asked enthusiastically, but didn't wait for an answer. She reached for her purse tucked beside her, snapped it open, and extracted a leather square about an inch thick. It was a small photo album. She opened it to the first page. "This is Donanne, my niece."

Mitch moved nearer and put his arm behind her along the back of the couch. "She's a beautiful girl. About G.T.'s age, isn't she?"

"They're two months apart. I was so surprised. Isn't it the greatest kind of luck that your aunt would have a child Donanne's age?"

"Do you get to see her often?" he asked.

"I do now." Anna hesitated. "My sister's...separated from her husband. They... She's back at home for a while."

"Will they get back together?" Mitch asked.

"I don't know. I don't think he's good for either of them."

"What does your sister think?"

Anna sighed. "She's confused, not sure of anything really."

"Show me another picture," he said, hoping to get her mind off her sister's troubles. He was successful and he could barely take his eyes off her animated happiness long enough to look at the photos. He'd never seen a woman look more lovely, more unreservedly delighted. He moved his hand to her shoulder, overcome by the temptation to touch her.

"This is Jamie."

Mitch glanced at the picture, then looked again and was startled. The dark-haired boy looked almost exactly like he had in his own baby pictures. "That could be me," he said, pointing.

Anna giggled. "He's a little shorter," she said.

Mitch smiled. "I didn't shave back then either."

"He is handsome, isn't he?"

"Hold that thought," Mitch said, got up, and crossed the room. He returned with a thick album and sat back down. "Just a minute, it's right..."—he turned several pages—"...right here."

"Oh, my. You and Jamie do look alike."

"Uh-huh," Mitch agreed, and put a finger on Jamie's picture. "Handsome devil," he said teasingly.

Anna looked at Mitch, then touched the face that was so close to hers. "Just like you are," she said softly.

"Anna..." He caught her hand and kissed the soft palm, then pressed it to his cheek. "You've given me so much pleasure in such a short time."

"I like being with you, too," she whispered.

His kiss was as soft as the fragrant cedar smoke that rose in the chimney, as warm as the scented air around them. It was unlike any kiss she'd ever had before, and she savored the gentleness of his lips. But it brought no peace to her heart. She felt as if she were trying to prepare a chocolate fondue without being tempted to take a taste. It couldn't be done. She wanted to know more of this new sweetness that tempted her.

She moved her head, almost imperceptibly, from side to side, and became acutely aware of the sensuous shape of his lips. The soft brushing motion was doing much more than satisfying her curiosity; it was warming her body, firing sensations deep within that threatened to overwhelm her. She pulled away from him, letting the hand he still held to his cheek slide from beneath his.

He smiled at her. "That was very nice," he said quietly, then closed the heavy album and removed it from his lap.

"*You're* very nice," she said, then tucked her pictures back into her purse. "But I'll bet you've heard that many times, haven't you?"

"I guess so," he said.

"You don't sound too happy about it."

He lifted an eyebrow. "It usually precedes a request," he said flatly.

"For what?"

"Whatever she wants at the moment."

Anna leaned away from him and smiled. "Now who's sounding bitter?" she asked.

Mitch smiled back. "I had that coming," he said. "So, now that I've paid the price, what shall I ask for?"

"What do you need?"

Anna closed her eyes, thought for a minute, then opened them. "I don't need anything. You can't teach me to make cinnamon toast, and my car's not broken. I don't want anything." She shrugged. "I guess you're off the hook."

"You are the most amazing woman I've ever known," he said.

"Would it make you feel better to know that I could use a really good recipe for *beurre blanc* with lemon?"

Mitch laughed. "I can't even spell it."

"Then you're a free man. How does it feel?"

"I guess I'll have to get used to it."

Anna could hear the pain in his voice, but she wasn't sure where it was coming from. "I didn't mean to bring up any bad memories," she said.

Mitch stared into the fire. "It isn't that," he said. "I'm just having a hard time understanding a woman like you."

She'd heard that before, but never in such a pleasant tone of voice. "That's probably because I'm confused, too," she said, trying to ease his discomfort.

"You are?" he asked, turning toward her.

She nodded.

"About us?"

"That, too," she said.

Mitch reached out to touch the high, modest collar

of her blouse again. Her elegant reserve fascinated him. "You're a proper lady, Anna."

"How proper would you have thought me if I'd told you I wanted a baby?" she asked.

The searing heat of desire flared through his body, and with it, the confusion returned. Since his divorce from Betina he'd been convinced that he would live his life both without a wife and without children. He was convinced that Betina's attempt to return to their marriage bed after he'd brought in the first oil well was motivated purely by greed on her part. Cynicism about all women had brought him no measure of comfort, but it had protected his heart. Now Anna had changed all that. She asked for nothing. The only thing she was greedy for was—

"*My* baby?" he asked.

"See, you'd have been shocked."

He'd been asked for practically everything else by the women in his life. He couldn't understand why this confounded him so. Maybe it was because there were no "strings" attached. That, in itself, threatened his ego. She needed nothing more than a tiny spark of life. Could he give her that and walk away?

But she hadn't even asked for that! "I'm more confused than shocked," he said finally.

"I understand," she said quietly. "A woman's desires must be very difficult for a man to feel."

"I'm not confused about what you want," he said. "The conflict is with me, with what I'm feeling."

"You'd want to be involved…as a parent, I mean. Is that it?"

Mitch closed his eyes in bewilderment. Where was his cool rationality now? he wondered. He'd said it himself; a friendship should be simple. A sexual relationship should be little more complicated. But this? He looked at her, the dilemma churning inside him.

"You don't have to explain," she said soothingly. "You're questioning my good sense, and I don't blame you. That's undoubtedly why I've never told anyone before," she finished thoughtfully.

Mitch put his arm around her shoulders again. "But you've told someone now. Why did you choose to tell me?" he asked.

Anna sighed. "I don't know." She hesitated.

Mitch felt his heartbeat accelerate, expecting the worst, or, at the very least, that she had no good reason at all. Did she think he was digging for a compliment?

"There are so many reasons," she continued, looking at him. "I've seen you having fun with George Thomas, and I know you care for children, so I thought you'd understand why I'd want to live with a child. I've heard you talk to Germaine about what a good job she's doing with George even though her husband is gone, so I knew you didn't have any qualms about a child being reared by one parent. There *is* a certain amount of prejudice toward single parents."

"You're probably right," Mitch said.

"You seem to be a very strong man, a man of experience who's seen a lot of the world. I can appreciate that, and I believe it builds tolerance to opposing views and ideas."

"You mean you wanted my opinion?" he asked.

Her head moved slowly from side to side. "I don't think so. Maybe it was just time to tell someone I felt very close to, someone I thought wouldn't be judgmental." She looked into the fireplace and sighed. "You seemed to care enough to listen."

Mitch guided her face back to his with a finger on her chin. "I care a lot more than that," he said.

Anna could feel something new and frightening happening to her well-organized reality. Up until now, a child of her own had been more of a hypothetical idea than a real possibility. She had kept herself restrained, waiting for that moment of truth to which she'd barely given any thought at all. She had to admit, no matter how much she wanted it, the child was merely a nebulous dream until—

Anna captured his hand and held it tightly. "I feel very nervous about all this, Mitch. Maybe I should never have said anything."

There was uncertainty in her voice and her expression. He wished that he could take it away, but he was as nervous as she was. "Don't be sorry that you told me, all right?"

"You're a good friend," she said, then realized

that she wanted to say so much more. Many nights she'd dreamed of how it would happen, and now the familiar, recurring dream sped through her mind in a fraction of a second. She and a faceless man would be walking down a city street, then stop in front of a tall, modern building. They would go inside and speak to a woman who leafed through the pages of a large book until she found Anna's name. When the woman was satisfied that Anna was in the book, she would direct them to a double door at the end of the hall.

Only the man was allowed through the doors, and when he returned he was carrying a beautiful, newborn baby. He would hand the baby to Anna, tell the woman to cross her name off the list, then disappear. Anna would wake up deliriously happy until she realized that there was no baby in her arms.

It was no longer possible to live with the unrealistic dream. Still clinging to his hand for courage, she leaned forward and kissed him lightly. "Maybe…maybe we could be more than friends," she murmured.

Mitch pulled her closer and felt the softness of her hair beneath his cheek while contradictory emotions tumbled one over another. "Anna," he breathed. "You're asking me to…make love to you."

Five

That was exactly what she'd asked. "Good heavens!" She dropped his hand and stood up. "I can't do that!"

Mitch caught the afghan as it fell from her lap, tossed it aside, and stood up to face her. "Anna, what's wrong?" He caught her by the waist before she could move away from him.

Anguish showed in the lines that marked her brow as she looked up at him. "I've put you in a terrible position. I...I wasn't thinking straight."

"What do you mean, not thinking straight?" he asked.

"You said you'd want to be involved...you

know…as a parent." She took a deep breath. "Mitch, I'm sorry."

He couldn't remember saying anything of the kind, but the memory of that part of their conversation came flooding back. When she'd asked the question, he'd been frightened and unsure of committing himself, and he actually evaded it by saying nothing. He hadn't answered because he honestly couldn't, while she'd gone on to assume that he was questioning her good sense by keeping silent. He still couldn't answer the question.

"Let's give it some time," he said.

Anna lowered her head. "Now I've made you feel obligated in some way. That was a very insensitive thing for me to do."

"Look at me, Anna." When she raised her head, there were tears shining in her eyes. Mitch swallowed with difficulty. "Dear Anna," he breathed. "No one could ever say that you're an insensitive person." He drew her into his arms and felt the lush ripeness of her body melt against him. Did she know the effect her nearness had on him? he wondered. Such innocence was rare.

They stood silently in the firelight, each one thinking private thoughts. For Anna it was a moment of truth. She'd ventured forth from her easy world of dreams into a difficult reality, a place of many perils. She hadn't known the dangers. Not that she feared for herself. Perhaps she should, though she felt no insecurity with her own goals. But she hadn't realized that involving the necessary other person could be so hazardous to his mental well-being. The chance of offending sensitive values had, unfortunately, never entered her mind. Her emotions were in chaos—she'd never been in love before.

Mitch was in the midst of utter conflict, also. The longer he held her, the greater was his desire to make love to her. He'd fantasized about it so often in the past few days that the very act of touching her meant another lesson in self-control. Yet, like her, he hadn't thought beyond a certain point in the scenes of passion that filled his mind. If it were possible, he'd loved her from those first few delightful moments when they'd shared a glass of sherry on her first night in Germaine's home.

It seemed so natural to kiss her, the shining aura of her hair a silken temptation. She was quiet in his arms, as his lips touched the fine strands, and the sweet, clean fragrance lifted his mind, like a narcotic, to a bright summer place. The smooth skin of her temple lured him, the line of her cheek a warm and rounded pleasure to explore. Entranced, his journey continued, the ripeness of her lips beckoning without speaking.

The moment electrified as Anna closed her eyes and lifted her chin. Her soft sigh seemed an invitation he couldn't decline. Had he really asked for time to think? he wondered, but couldn't remember. The thought to comfort her fled in the wake of his desire.

Anna was aware of the consolation he'd tried to give her. She'd even thought to thank him before she excused herself to go to bed. Crossing the line into the realm of erotic pleasures didn't occur to her until it was too late to be wary. Her hands came to rest lightly on his waist, but it wasn't enough. She had to know him, to feel the taut muscles, the exotic flare of his male form as her hands moved higher.

Her hands faltered, then resumed their search, and the power of his body became apparent, while a contrasting weakness invaded her own. Sensations, new to her, stole conviction away. She was too warm, yet she trembled. She wanted to speak, yet she remained silent.

He tasted of sweet confections, enticing concoctions, the recipes totally unknown, never learned. She could place no restrictions on sampling the delicacy, as her senses filled with the delicious feast. His tongue touched the corner of her mouth, then brushed the line between her lips, and a sample was no longer enough.

She wanted to become a connoisseur, the only authority on the overpowering delectability of the man in her arms. Her lips parted and volatile hungers met, combining rich and exotic spices. The intoxicating mixture was so new and unfamiliar that she'd never realized it should be included. Now it seemed indispensable, thrilling her with discoveries, filling her body with the essence of celebration.

Her artless hunger overwhelmed him. From one second to the next, he was surprised by her response. But when her arms tightened about him and drew him closer, he lost the capability to analyze. He knew nothing but the craving that consumed him. Her hands would move, new sparks would flash. He felt strong fingers grasping, not meaning to coax, but searching for a place to cling. They moved beneath his arms, relinquishing his back to smooth over his chest, then rose to his shoulders. Her palm pressed against the back of his head, and eager lips increased the pressure until he was breathless.

There had been choices to make, and he fought to remember them. His heart would be with her always. It would be impossible. He couldn't deceive her.

"I can't do this," he breathed, his lips touching her cheek. He felt her body tense, then lean toward him, as if all her energy had been drained away.

Shocked, Anna turned her face toward the fire. She took one breath, then two. "I understand," she whispered.

Mitch pressed her head to his chest and held her tightly. "No, you don't," he said.

"It would be a responsibility," she said.

"Just the opposite," he countered.

She didn't care that she didn't know what he

meant. She'd had enough confusion for one night. "Promise me something," she said.

"What?"

She twisted in his arms, putting a necessary space between them, then looked at him. "Promise that we'll never talk about this again."

"No. I won't promise that."

She pulled away from him. "I insist," she said.

"That's your privilege."

She turned and reached for her purse, then looked back. "Thank you for inviting me to Santino's. I enjoyed your music."

"Anna..." She was around the love seat and moving toward the door before he could say anything else. Just as well. He had no idea what to say now anyway.

She hurried up the stairs, down the carpeted hall, and into the serenity of her room. In minutes she was out of her clothes and into a cooling shower. She hoped that she could soon escape into sleep and leave the horrible embarrassment behind. In his arms, she'd forgotten about the baby she so desperately wanted. She'd wanted the man, and now her body flushed with remembering.

The question was: How could that be? She was not a complete stranger to passion, but she had never felt anything like the wanton behavior she'd exhibited tonight. Lust, the sequel of love? she wondered. Or was it the other way around—love, the consequence of desire? Her ignorance of the subject angered her. Too bad she hadn't the aptitude for making such useful discoveries before the knowledge was needed, she thought ruefully, as she dried herself.

But serendipity had eluded her, and she was further away from her goal than ever before. She looked with contempt at the full-length, voluminous, batiste of the nightgown that hung on the inside of the closet door. The tiny embroidered amber flowers mocked her, the somber muted peach of the background fitted her mood, the narrow ruffles at the cuffs and high collar seemed a sham after the way she'd behaved this night. Red satin, décolletage—that would have been more fitting.

She hurried to cover herself with the offending cotton garment. To her surprise, it felt more comfortable than it ever had, and she relished the buttoning of each tiny pearl. This was the Anna she knew, reserved, modest—alone.

Mitch didn't know how long he'd stared into the fire. The only move he'd made since Anna had left the room was to pull off his boots and prop his feet up on the hearth. The flame was dying, and he hadn't made a move to stir it back to life. He felt as if the embers were smoldering in his stomach. He had a scar on his arm where a branding iron had seared him. The hurt had been less painful than the rejection he was feeling right now. Worse, the rejection was the result of his own indecision.

Analyzing was fine if one was looking at a piece of property, studying soil samples and terrain, purchasing a horse of good blood. Shouldn't making love be an easier decision to make? he wondered. It always had been before. The only thing he'd needed to know was the cost, whether or not a trap was being set.

He'd avoided a trap once. The woman had wanted him and thought to snare him in the web of fatherhood. Now he was imprisoned outside that delicate web. The pain of it wrenched through him, leaving him with a tremor of fear.

Of course, it was possible that Anna had the same thing in mind, but he would never have thought of the tactic she was using. He sat up straight. How clever she was, he thought. How very brilliant an idea to tempt with the forbidden, to taunt with the impossible. Didn't the rarity of an object increase its worth? Wouldn't any male be damned before he'd give up such a valuable prize?

He was off the couch and pacing, the words repeating in his mind. Not Anna, no...not my Anna. She'd told him the truth; he knew it. She wanted nothing, she needed nothing. He stopped pacing and looked toward the door. But she'd wanted *him*—and he'd denied her.

He walked into the dimly lit entry hall and looked up the stairs. Could he go to her now, and later walk away from his own child? He thought of the home he'd vowed never to leave. He thought of Anna's ties with her family. Perhaps he could convince her later that the child needed a father. Perhaps he could become the man she'd want for a husband.

If he tried to explain the dilemma to Joey, he'd be laughed out of the room. "I'm sure I've walked away from a few and didn't even know it, old buddy," he'd probably say. "Ideal situation, old buddy," he'd probably say. But then Mitch had never been in the habit of talking about personal things with anyone, so Joey's reaction was nothing but hypothesis.

Mitch put a hand on the banister, one foot on the first step, and slumped forward. He felt exhausted with questions. Had he considered them all? he wondered. Was there anything left to ask? Yes!

If not me, then who?

The mantle of tiredness slipped from him, and he bounded up the stairs three at a time. He came to a stop outside her door, lifted his hand to knock, then let it drop. It had to be at least four o'clock in the morning. A disturbance was out of the question. Would she still be awake? he wondered, as he entered his room and crossed diagonally to their common door. He tapped softly. No answer.

He tapped again, waited, and was about to turn away when he heard a creaking sound. She was opening the door to the hallway. He knocked again, louder this time.

"Anna?" He heard the other door close, the click of the light switch. "Anna?"

"What's wrong?"

"Nothing...everything. I have to talk to you."

"No."

"It can't wait," he said.

"It will have to wait, Mitch."

"I'm going to open this door and say what I have to say." He knew instantly that he'd chosen the wrong tack.

"And that will be your last trip through either door into my room, Mitchell McCabe," she said.

He closed his eyes, inhaled slowly, exhaled slowly. "Please."

Anna could picture him on the other side of the door. By now, she knew him well enough to realize that he would not want to give up. He would keep on trying. She sighed. "Open the door, Mitch," she said. And she heard the key turn a second later.

"You have one minute," she said as he came in.

He looked around as she crossed to one of the chairs in the corner. A tiny, silk-shaded night lamp on top of a chest near the door was the only illumination. He could feel her presence in the room; the flowery fragrance she wore surrounded him. He looked toward her and began to worry that he wouldn't be able to speak. Curled up in the big over-stuffed chair, waiting, she was the most beautiful creature he'd ever seen.

She touched the top button of her gown. "Your time is running out, Mr. McCabe," she said, then watched as he moved away from the small circle of dim light. He knelt down in front of her, his face a beautiful mixture of angled shadow and dark plane.

"I want to make love to you, Anna," he said softly.

If her legs hadn't been tucked beneath her, she would have been out of the chair and across the room in a second. *Why didn't I stand at the door?* she wondered futilely. "Please don't do this, Mitch," she said, her tone pleading.

"I *want* to do this."

"You don't know what you're saying," she challenged.

"Yes, I do."

"You've changed your mind, then?" she asked.

"No. I've made up my mind."

"That's hard to believe in such a short time," she said.

"It's true, just the same," he said.

"No matter what happens, you won't interfere?"

"I'll do whatever you want," he hedged.

"No one is to know," she said.

"Unless you choose to tell them," he said.

Her hand went to the top button again. *Is this really happening, or am I dreaming it?* She closed her eyes, then felt his hand touch her leg.

"Anna?"

She looked at him, and all the yearning she'd felt before returned. There was only one thing to say. "Yes."

Before she knew what was happening, he'd lifted her into his arms. "You look like an angel, Anna. A sweet and beautiful angel." He crossed to the bed, but he didn't put her down. Instead, he sat on the edge, cradling her. "I have to tell you one more thing, all right?"

She nodded. His voice was a mere whisper, and she felt his breath against her cheek as he spoke.

"I love you."

Then his lips covered hers, and she could feel his arms tightening around her. There had never been a kiss like this one, lingering, tasting, until she thought that nothing more wonderful could happen. She was wrong. His tongue gently parted her lips, exploring, touching, searching deeper for sweet tastes. Her fingers slipped into his thick, dark hair and she held him, keeping his mouth on hers, wanting the kiss to continue.

Her appetite grew. She could feel the hardness of his legs beneath her, and when he moved, a tiny sob of delight rose in her throat. The sound frightened her. She was a novice in the realm of an expert. Her reactions were those of a neophyte, and he should be told lest he be disappointed.

But she couldn't speak. He'd freed his hand from beneath her legs to let her weight rest in his lap. Each tiny button that she'd so carefully fastened was being slowly undone. His arm moved between her breasts, as his fingers descended from one closure to the next.

She felt a desperate need to run away. No man had ever looked upon her naked flesh.

Mitch felt her trembling. The last of many buttons was free, and his own hand shook with the excitement of discovery. But he wanted to go slowly, he wanted to give her more pleasure than she'd ever had in the arms of another. His fingers smoothed over the soft material of her gown, the ripeness of her breast filling his hand. Then she turned, her arms around his neck, and clung to him.

She seemed almost pristine. Holding herself tightly against him, it was as if she were afraid to be touched. Could it possibly be that she had never made love before? The idea astonished him and splintered his thoughts like light cutting through a prism. How could he ease her fear?

"This was my parents' marriage bed," he said softly.

The pressure of her hold loosened. "I remember," she said.

"My mother was frightened, too," he said.

"How do you know?"

"My father told me."

She touched his cheek and looked into his dark eyes. There was kindness there, perhaps taught by his caring parent. "Your father loves you very much."

He caught her hand, kissed the tips of her fingers, then pressed them to the top button of his shirt. "Will you help me?" he asked. She hesitated. "Please."

Each small disk seemed an insurmountable obstacle. What should have been an easy task became more and more difficult as tremors of doubt flowed through her fingers. She stopped at the lowest button she could reach without moving away from him.

"Touch me, Anna." As he spoke, he guided her hand inside his shirt and pressed her palm to his chest.

She thought to pull it away, but the wondrous male contours and textures enticed her. Her hand moved by itself; she no longer needed his persuasion. The shape and feel of him thrilled and fascinated her as she brushed sensitive fingers over the crisp hair that curled on his chest. The skin on his shoulders felt like satin to her touch, the muscles beneath, a powerful force kept in check by the fragile covering.

"You're a beautiful man," she murmured, then looked up into his eyes. "But you know that, don't you?"

He didn't answer her question. "I want to know your beauty, Anna," he said instead. Tentatively, he moved his hand to her breast. "May I touch you?" Taking her silence as an answer, he pushed the soft material of her gown aside. The sharp intake of her breath stopped his hand at the outer curve of her breast.

"Do you know how lovely you are?" he asked.

Anna closed her eyes, her breath still trapped inside her chest.

"Look at my hand, Anna."

Exhaling slowly, she opened her eyes. Deeply tanned fingers looked even darker in the shadowy light. Next to the whiteness of her bosom, his hand seemed a potent force, the contrast more exciting than she could have imagined. She raised her eyes to his, and his hand began to move, gently describing the heavy, rounded curves.

"Now you know how I see you."

In a moment, her gown was being pushed from her shoulders, and she felt the light cloth slide down her back and arms. Then she seemed to be suspended in the air as he leaned to the side and eased her onto the pillows. Ruffly cuffs were tugged over her hands, and in one smooth motion, the gown was gone, and Mitch stood beside the bed towering over her.

The words he meant to speak caught in his throat as he gazed down at her. He'd wanted to reassure her, but her innocent beauty had captured his tongue. Reclining against the soft down on the many pillows, she looked like a timorous princess awaiting the first touch of an unknown prince. Her eyes were wide with apprehension, dark with disquiet.

What was it he was going to say to comfort her? He wondered, but couldn't remember. "Do you want me to turn out the light?" he asked instead.

Anna gathered her courage. "No. I want to see the father of my child."

He thought his body might burst, spontaneously, into flame. When she rose to kneel before him, reaching out to finish unbuttoning his shirt, a violent inner trembling threatened to undo his senses. Her hands moved slowly across his chest, brushing sensitive nipples, causing him to catch his breath, as she pushed his shirt from his shoulders.

He watched, her hands sure in their task now. When he felt his shirt being pulled from beneath his belt, he tried to relax. Her expertise had probably been earned; no doubt she'd dressed and undressed all manner of children. But the sight of her lush body moving before him kept him tense with anticipation. Her full bosom rose and fell with each breath, and she seemed to be completely unaware of the erotic display as her arms pressed, then released, the rounded curves.

His belt and trousers were undone, and Anna was moving her hands around his waist. When they met at the center of his back, she stopped, tensed. With a quiet sigh, she pushed down on the heavy leather of his belt, then looked away. She heard the rustling of cloth, and when she looked back, his tanned body wore nothing but white cotton briefs.

Her shyness gave him a little courage. Cupping her face in his hands, he kissed her, then wrapped his arms around her. "You're not finished," he whispered.

Anna could feel the curling hair on his chest pressing against her breasts, and as his hands moved down her back to draw her closer, she became acutely aware of the hard secret still hiding from her. Even in a house full of brothers, she'd never seen the glory of a man's arousal. "I can't," she breathed, her eyes averted.

He kissed the top of her head. "I'm going to be the father of our child," he said.

Our child? She'd always thought of the baby as being totally hers. Suddenly, stunningly, she knew that it would never be so. "Your baby will be as beautiful as you are," she said softly.

"Then know me, Anna. Know me well...like you've never known another man."

She looked up at him. "I've never..." Her hands withdrew from his shoulders and crossed at the base of her neck. Her arms chastely covered her breasts, her hands atop one another on her chest. "I haven't known..." She looked away as she pulled out of his arms.

The next moment he was beside her, lifting, helping her to lie back, and in the space of that moment, he'd removed the last garment between them. He lay on his side, propped on one elbow, his hand behind the base of her neck. His head lowered, and their lips met, but only for a fleeting moment. His kisses followed a wandering hand, touching places that had never been touched before.

Gentle lips outlined the curve of each breast, then found the sensitive valley between. When his mouth brushed one pale, centered circle, Anna gasped in disbelief. None of the sensations were familiar. She felt electrified, on fire. His tongue licked across her nipple; then he drew the growing peak into his mouth.

She'd never imagined that she could feel like this. Her fingers clutched at his body, and muted little cries escaped as the pleasure overwhelmed her. The tugging at her breast intensified the hunger growing deep within her. His hand was searching for the hunger, and a pooling of moist warmth gathered to astound her as his fingers touched the center of the flame.

"No," she cried out softly.

"Yes," was the answer to her protest.

His leg moved over hers and kept her from pulling away from him. For a moment she felt trapped and anxious, but gentle fingers coaxed her, spreading the warmth, communicating the tenderness he felt with every circling touch. The anxiety was transformed to wonder, and desire spiraled through her body as the search moved inside her.

"No," she said again, but she was breathless with wanting him to continue.

"I don't want to hurt you," he whispered.

She pushed the thought of pain aside as she arched against his palm. Her hands reached out, urging him to move toward her, over her. "Please…" She could barely catch her breath. "Love me."

He didn't resist her; he couldn't. He'd been at the edge of control for what seemed like forever. At last he was at the threshold of ecstasy and barely able to slow his entry into paradise—but he knew he must. He cared nothing for the noble thoughts of fatherhood now; his only goal was to love the woman of his dreams and earn her love in return.

As slowly as his hunger would allow, he lowered his body towards hers. Every muscle was tense with the fear that he would hurt her. It wasn't fair to put this angelic woman through a difficult initiation to loving.

A tentative touch was all the invitation Anna needed. He felt her hands move along his sides, past his waist, then lower, until she could pull him toward her. She arched urgently upward, the partial joining making her fingers dig wantonly into firm muscle.

"Slowly," he warned.

"No."

"Anna!" he gasped. But it was too late. His strength for resisting was gone.

He captured her cry in a kiss, the plaintive sound making his body flare with hunger and his mind reel in penitence. But he was powerless to stop loving her, helpless in his desperate need.

A spring of womanly knowledge bubbled inside her, teaching her what to do even as she received him. The unknown rhythms suffused her mind and guided her body in perfect harmony with his. His strength refined her softness and clarified the reflection of her ecstasy in his loving eyes.

But then she could no longer see him. Her eyes

closed against the brilliant flash of fire that stabbed at her. She heard two helpless cries of delight and knew it was her own sound that blended with the jubilant baritone. She was breathless, her kisses randomly placed with each shuddering sigh.

He couldn't stop saying her name. It carried into the air on every breath and echoed a song he would never forget.

"Anna..."

Six

"**A**nna…please don't cry."

Tears shone in her eyes and glistened on her cheeks, but she smiled at him. "Am I crying?" she asked, teasing.

Mitch kissed away one of the sparkling droplets, then touched her lips with his. "You're crying," he said softly. "Tell me why."

Anna wiped at the corner of her eye. "I've never felt this happy before," she said, as if the information should have been self-evident.

Mitch moved to his side and tugged at the quilts on the bed. With Anna's help, they pulled the coverings down over them. He propped himself on an elbow and looked at her. "Now tell me that again," he said.

"I'm happy," she said simply.

Her eyes were glowing, just as they had been when she'd talked of the children she loved. He was afraid to pursue the cause of her happiness now for fear of learning that only his potential to father a child was the catalyst and not he, alone. He placed his hand gently on her abdomen. "Are you all right?" he asked.

"I don't think I've ever been better," she said, gazing contentedly into his eyes.

"I didn't want to hurt you," he said softly, his thumb beginning to rub the smooth skin at her waist.

Anna reached out to touch his face, her fingers moving along the line of his jaw. "I've already forgotten about that." Her hand moved to the back of his neck, and she drew him toward her. "Kiss me again," she whispered.

His lips brushed hers lightly, but it wasn't nearly enough. Now that she'd had a taste of loving, her appetite had grown a hundredfold. Not in her wildest imagination would she have thought that it would be so. Her fingers slipped into his hair, and she held him closer, relishing the pressure of his mouth, the feel of his warm breath on her cheek.

Mitch turned so that his upper body was over hers, his arms holding him slightly above her. He couldn't help but be surprised by the affection she was showing. His experience with virginal women was limited to one other, and that had been a disastrous episode at the age of seventeen, when both parties had been without previous knowledge and each had failed miserably. The girl had never spoken to him again, and his young ego had taken months to repair. He had nothing by which to gauge Anna's reaction except that one nightmarish memory.

But Anna was obviously not a frightened schoolgirl. Neither was she apprehensive any longer. Something had transformed a celibate child-woman into a sensuous goddess. Reluctantly, he pulled away from her delicious kiss when she pressed on his shoulder.

"Mitch?"

"Yes."

"You don't work tomorrow night, do you?"

"No," he said.

"Let's do something really special tomorrow."

"It's tomorrow right now," he reminded her. And they'd already done the most special thing he could imagine, he thought.

"A picnic," she said.

He gave her a quick kiss. "That's special, all right," he said agreeably.

She cupped his face in both hands. "Not as special as you are," she said softly.

"That's the nicest thing anybody's ever said to me, Anna."

"How about this? 'You're a genius, cowboy,'" she teased, echoing Carolyn's earlier words.

"I'd rather be special to you," he said.

She turned on her side to face him and looked into his eyes. "So special," she whispered, then lured him into another kiss.

Strange patterns mixed and mismatched in her mind. She should be thinking of the child, but all she wanted to think about was the man lying beside her, facing her. Surely there was an explanation. She touched his chest, then let her hand roam, memorizing form and curve and plane. Temptation conquered shyness, and her hand moved down his side to the narrow waist. There were so many things to learn—important things.

"Were you happy, too?" she asked.

"Yes."

"Happy…enough?" she asked hesitantly.

He put a hand on the roundness of her hip. "What are you asking me, Anna?"

"If…everything was…all right," she said shyly.

"Is that important to you?"

He had every right to ask the question. Under these very odd circumstances he had every reason to believe that he was being used. But, curiously, his feelings were more important to her than she could have imagined they would be. "Yes, it is," she said.

Her answer was an exquisite ray of hope, but it was much too early to stake his happiness on such fragile blessings. "I will never forget you, Anna," he said.

He was already saying goodbye. His poignant tone pierced her heart, and her sense of loss was profound. She didn't want to think of their parting. What was there to say after being given such a glorious compliment? she wondered. Second thoughts made her hesitate to return it in the same manner. She couldn't bring herself to say goodbye. "Thank you," she said quietly.

Suddenly, it seemed even more important to know him, the feel of his body, the sound of his voice, his needs, wishes, and dreams. Still facing him, her hand moved automatically away from his waist, over his hard, lean hip, along the firm length of his thigh that was angled toward her. "I love touching you." Her hand stopped. "I didn't know I would," she said, looking up at him.

"Are you surprised?" he asked.

"Very pleasantly," she said.

Two glimmers of hope were two more than he'd hoped for. "I'm glad," he said. His hand moved from the lush curve of her hip to rest just above her waist. He could feel the outline of her ribs, the slow movement caused by her breathing. The tip of his thumb touched the underside of her breast, and he felt like throwing back the quilts to look upon the beauty he remembered. His hands became a substitute for his eyes.

What a beautiful mother this child will have, he thought, as he traced the generous curve. *God! How I want to be there with her, to care for her, to watch my child grow within her*, he thought. As she lay on her side, the division between her breasts was like a soft trap, the velvet of her skin pressing against his fingers from both sides. His heart ached. Only his baby would get to see her; only his baby would get to suckle at her ripe bosom.

The nipples rose to greet him as he touched one and then the other. His finger circled, and the bud blossomed further. His mind wandered into the future, and he could see Anna as her figure changed, her smile when she saw the newborn infant for the first time, her contentment with the baby at her breast. Perhaps she was right, he thought. Perhaps the child would need only to be loved by this woman, who had so much love to give.

It was such sweet torture to lie beside her. Already, he could feel the stirrings of passion again. The light touch of her hand, as it moved over his body, was tempting him. *Don't let my eagerness push her away*, he warned himself. But he needn't have worried.

Anna could barely believe what was happening to her, and she had no idea of how to get what she wanted. Inexperience made her hesitant, and the simplest answer, to ask, seemed the most fraught with danger. Contradictions flooded her mind. She'd never thought of herself as angelic, but Mitch apparently had, and her hunger for him seemed anything but chaste.

How wonderful his rugged body felt to her exploring hand. How she longed to feel strong arms holding her again. His hand at her breast sent shafts of fire through her body and made her tremble with longing. Did he know? Two fingers closed over a sensitive nipple, and the tender rolling and twisting made her gasp with wonder, her body arching toward the source of the sweet agony.

The quilts slipped down to her waist, and she knew a moment of concern. The old modesty fought for control, but she was helpless to assist the false value. She felt his arm slide behind her back, then reveled in the strength that held her captive.

"Your body is so lovely, Anna," Mitch whispered. "The perfect place for a baby to grow."

His fingers described the curves he saw, and the feathery touch heightened the sensitivity of her heated skin. She could feel the swelling and marveled at her body's response. When his lips touched where his hand had been, she wanted to cry out with joy, and she cradled him close as they closed over one jutting nipple.

He drew her into his mouth, and the cry could no longer be contained within her feverish body. Each tug on the delicate bud brought forth a gasp of pleasure that she couldn't control. The torment was exquisite.

"Stop!" Her fingers dug into the muscle of his thigh. "No, don't stop…yes, do."

Mitch kissed the distended nipple, then brushed his lips across the tip. "I'm confused," he murmured.

Anna could hear the smile in his voice. "Me, too," she said breathlessly.

He raised his head and looked down at her, his eyes twinkling with pleasure. "Then we both have a problem. What's yours?"

She shook her head. "I…don't know what to say."

"I do," he whispered.

"What?"

"I want you, Anna."

Her eyes widened. "You do?"

He placed his hand atop hers and began moving it up his thigh. She realized he wanted to *show* her that he was speaking the truth. Startled, she pulled her hand away, then instantly regretted her cowardice. But Mitch seemed to understand, and there were no reprisals, verbal or otherwise. He simply drew her closer and kissed her.

But she did want to know, and her body pressed toward him. It was true, and she felt his hand descend to pull her nearer, tighter against his unyielding passion. She ached to feel the overpowering fullness again, the bounty that could bring inordinate satiety.

"Please," she said, breathing heavily, and held him tightly as insistent hands encouraged his body to cover hers.

There was no cry of pain this time, only a duet of soft and ecstatic singing, the harmony preserved in her mind as a perfect blending of tonal flavors. His extravagance completed her, integrating some lost part of her life into a unifying whole, and with every velvet charge she knew the meaning of perfect synergy.

"I love you." The words escaped before she had time to consider them, but once released from the prison of her heart, they became an integral part of her being. An unbearable tension began to build, as if the words were creating a wild and excessive plethora of exotic sensations that engorged her body with lavish power.

The confession flooded his body with energy, and the procession of three little words through his consciousness set free the throbbing deluge of desire. Mitch felt that he was teetering on the edge of sanity, transcending the essence of mere pleasure, crossing a boundary into complete bliss.

"My love...my Anna."

The melody of his voice washed through her as the seed of his love filled the aching hunger within her. Captivated, and completely disarmed, she clung to him, worshipping his power to enthrall her. His ragged breathing tantalized her and matched the rhythm of her own. She felt drugged with the warmth of his skin, immersed in plenitude.

Their breathing slowed, and the once maddening

hunger abated. Mitch started to lift his weight from her, but she held him, enjoying the heavy prison of his body.

"Don't go."

He gave her a reassuring kiss, then moved to his side. "I'm not going anywhere," he said.

She turned into his arms. "You'll stay the night?" she asked.

He smiled. "The night is over."

She touched his smiling lips with a finger. "I don't believe you."

"Take a look," he said.

Anna raised herself, using his shoulder as a lever, and looked toward the eastern windows. The sun shimmered in the narrow slit between the shade and the frame, diffusing into intricate patterns through the heavy lace curtain. "You're right," she said. "The sun is— Oh!"

Mitch had resisted temptation as long as he could. Her slender midriff glowed ivory-white before him, her abundant breasts swaying seductively as she moved to see past him. His teeth nipped at the creamy plane of skin. Then he began to nuzzle beneath the heavy globes, his lips nibbling at the extravagant fullness.

"The sun is what?" he asked teasingly, then resumed his curious probing.

"The sun—Mitch!" The roughness of his beard

grazed between her breasts, the tender bite of his kisses following the valley between.

"You were saying?" he encouraged, as he nudged one delicious curve, then let the indentation round to its previous fullness.

"You're not listening to me," she said with mock severity.

"I'm just waiting for you to tell me what time it is," he said.

His hot breath flowed over one tender nipple as he spoke, his lips just a whisper away from the capture. Anna slipped her hand between his teasing mouth and her breast, then kissed the top of his head. "Picnic time," she said into the tousled darkness.

Mitch nipped at the fingers that cupped her bosom. "Not fair," he said, looking up at her. "You've interrupted a very important mission."

"And what was that?" she asked, sliding down to face him.

"Reconnaissance."

"The only place you're going to explore this morning is the kitchen," she said sternly.

His smile was sly. "But I need to know the teacher better," he whined.

"She'll overlook your lack of knowledge, I'm sure."

"But will she forgive it?"

"You can ask her that later," she assured him. "But *after* your lesson."

Mitch tucked his arm behind her back and pulled her closer. "What will I learn today?" he asked.

"Restraint?" Anna asked, teasing.

"And just who's going to teach me that?" he chuckled.

"Me?" she questioned.

"Not qualified," he said.

She leaned away from him. "What do you mean, not qualified?" But she knew exactly what he meant.

His only answer was a smile.

"I think I'm going to have to be very strict in the classroom," she said.

"Then I'd better behave myself, hadn't I?"

She grinned at him. "You wouldn't dare."

He wrapped her in his arms and relaxed beside her. Neither one moved nor spoke, and the silence of the rising sun finally lulled them into slumber. It was almost noon when Anna awoke to find Mitch standing at the south windows looking down into the garden. He wore only his trousers and looked like a bronze god in the slanting sunlight.

"You're awake," she said sleepily. "Have you been up long?"

He turned from the window. "Just a few minutes." *Long enough to know that I never want to leave this room as long as you're in it,* he thought sadly.

She wanted him to come to her and kiss her good-morning, but he stayed where he was. "Are you having second thoughts about your cooking lesson?'' she asked.

He moved to the foot of the bed and grasped the high post. ''You'll go easy on me, won't you?''

''I'll be reasonable,'' she said.

Mitch realized his tension was making her uncomfortable. ''That's fair,'' he said, smiling. ''Are you ready to get started?''

''Think I'll get dressed first,'' she said.

''That's disappointing,'' he said seriously.

She tossed a pillow at him. ''I'll knock on your door when I'm out of the shower,'' she said.

''I could help.''

She arced another pillow at his chest. ''See that door?'' She pointed across the room and he glanced back. ''Use it, cowboy.''

Mitch touched his fingers to his lips, then blew her a kiss. ''Teachers can be mighty tough, can't they?''

''Git!''

As soon as Mitch had left the room, Anna got up and went into the bathroom. The warm shower felt good, and even with just such a short rest, she found herself full of energy and looking forward to seeing Mitch again as soon as possible. Her hair was dry and she had put on a light touch of makeup in record time, but her impatience was arrested by what she saw in the long mirror of the dressing table as she took off her robe.

Her body seemed to be glowing with the pleasure

Mitch had given her. Her breasts were no longer just a part of her body; they were a curving avenue of pleasure, both hers and his. She put her hand flat on her stomach and imagined that his child was already growing within her. The dream that used to be merely an abstraction was now a whisper away from reality. She could feel that exciting fountain of need well inside her, threatening her reserve, and she imagined herself dressed in the red satin gown she'd denounced as lascivious.

She could barely recognize the thoughts as her own. Where was the chaste and proper lady who once resided in this newly liberated body? she wondered, as she stepped into tan corduroy trousers and tucked in the long-sleeved, high-collared beige sweater. She had the urge to pull the demure sweater off and exchange it for a blouse that she could unbutton to a libidinous level. *Be rational!* she scolded herself, stepping into flat shoes, then fastening her belt before she could change her mind about her first choice of clothing.

Only a door stood between her and the one person she most wanted to see, but she couldn't knock on it immediately. It was too soon, she thought. No. Her hesitation stemmed from Mitch's strange languor. It had been almost as if he were avoiding her. She didn't feel indecent, but he could be thinking it of her. She turned and leaned heavily against the frame.

Was he felling tricked? Compromised? Seduced?

Why shouldn't he? she asked herself, and debated leaving La Maison. *Please don't let it be true,* she pleaded silently, then straightened, put on a smile, and knocked on the door.

"Come."

She caught her breath when she saw him. He sat on the edge of an overstuffed chair wearing only a pair of jeans and one sock. The muscles of his arms and bare, furred chest rippled as he tugged at the other. His hair was still damp from the shower, and dark, curling wisps clung to his forehead and temples. *My eyes can't get enough of him, either,* she thought shamelessly. "You're a beautiful sight," she said, approaching the chair.

He looked up, down, then up again. "And so are you. Come here." He held out his hand, took hers, and drew her down into his lap. "Are you sure you want to wear that in the same kitchen with me?" he asked, smiling.

"Is that fair warning?"

"Never could get the hang of an eggbeater," he said.

"I brought an apron." She circled a finger on his chest. "It might save part of you." She drew a square, the sides just touching the outside of each nipple. "I can't guarantee the rest." Her hand brushed outside the imaginary square.

"I could wear an old shirt," he suggested.

"Or none at all," she said.

"After you refused the same suggestion? That wouldn't be fair, now, would it?"

Anna leaned against him and brushed at the wayward strands of his damp hair. "What's fair?" she asked, then saw the muscles of his jaw tighten.

"Not much," he said.

She kissed his cheek and pushed herself out of his lap. "You're stalling," she said.

"On the contrary." Mitch bent forward and reached for his boots. "I was being held captive," he said as he pulled them on. He stood. "Well, what's it to be—old shirt, new shirt?"

"Washable," she answered.

He grabbed the shirt that was hanging on the bedpost and put it on.

Anna stepped up to him and began doing the buttons.

He watched for a moment, then couldn't stand it any longer. His hands stayed hers, and she looked up at him. "Don't spoil me, Anna," he said softly.

Her hands dropped from his and she looked down at the floor. "I'm sorry." She turned and started back toward the door.

"Wait." His arms were around her waist, and he pulled her tightly against him. "I shouldn't have said that."

"You should say what you feel," she said.

"No...I shouldn't."

"You're wanting to forget about our agreement," she said.

"No." He turned her around to face him. "Don't even think such a thing."

"But you're uncomfortable with it," she challenged.

"Is that so strange?" he asked.

She leaned against him, thankful for his honesty and for his strength. "I guess no," she said.

He held her until she pushed away. "You think the kitchen is ready for us?" he asked lightly.

She tried a smile. "Might as well go see."

"Ahrrgg! What's that smell?" George Thomas's voice rose above the whir of the blender, and the grimace on his face told the story of olfactory distress.

"Why aren't you in school, cowboy?" Mitch asked.

"It's afternoon," G.T. said. Then he looked up and realized who was in the kitchen. "Did you make that?" He pinched his nose.

Mitch crouched down to G.T.'s level. "Just a little pot trouble, partner. Nothing I can't handle."

"Did my mother say you could boil all over her stove?" G.T. asked suspiciously.

Germaine appeared at the door with a smile on her face. "It's for his own good, child. Miss Anna is giving him a cooking lesson."

"Not eggs!" G.T. said plaintively.

"Something much better," Mitch said, and he gave G.T. a hug.

"Will I like it?"

"Well, let's see." Mitch lifted the boy and brought him to the counter where Anna was stirring a fragrant mixture of diced ham, olives, and pasta shells. "We have a brave man here," Mitch said. "He wants to taste my conchili."

"Conchigle," Anna corrected.

"With ham," Mitch added, dipping a spoon into the bowl.

G.T. nuzzled the pasta in cautious fashion, then licked at the corners of his mouth. "Mmm." He tipped the spoon, devoured the contents, and chewed thoughtfully. After a moment, he fixed Mitch with a suspicious stare. "You didn't make that," he said.

"Bet I did," Mitch challenged.

"Miss Anna made it," G.T. insisted.

"He really did make it, G.T.," Anna said.

"Then why do I like it?" G.T. asked seriously.

Anna kissed the boy's cheek. "Because it tastes good," she said.

"Oh."

"Time for a rest, George Thomas," Germaine said.

"Can I have a drink of water?"

Anna got him one.

"Can I have a snack?"

Anna reached into the cookie jar, brought out two fat oatmeal cookies, and handed them to him.

"Can I have a—"

"Nap," Germaine interrupted.

"I haven't eaten my cookies," G.T. said.

"Let's see if you can walk and eat at the same time," Germaine teased.

Mitch lowered him to the floor and gave his behind a loving pat.

"How come short cowboys have to take naps and big ones don't?" G.T. asked.

"What do you mean? I had a nap this morning myself," Mitch said, then glanced sideways at Anna. Her cheeks suffused with color in the most charming way, and she turned back to her stirring.

"You took a nap?" G.T. asked in disbelief.

"Well, when you get plumb worn out, that's what you have to do," Mitch explained.

"Okay," G.T. said, and took a bite of his cookie with his first step toward the door.

"Plumb worn out, were you?" Anna chided when they were alone again.

Mitch moved behind her and put his hands on her hips. "Not anymore," he said suggestively.

Anna looked back at him. "Well, good. You'll have enough energy to put this in the thermos while it's still warm, then."

"Yes, ma'am, teacher, ma'am." He took a step back and came to attention. "Filling the thermos, ma'am."

Seven

―――

"This is a perfect place," Anna said, gazing into the distance where young children played around swings and teeter-totters.

"I thought you might like it." Mitch put the picnic basket on one of the tables and sat down.

"This must be their favorite place," Anna said thoughtfully.

He knew she was referring to the children. "I always liked it," Mitch said.

Anna sat down beside him and leaned back against the table also. "You did very well in the kitchen today," she said.

"You were patient," he said.

"That's not the reason, silly," she said.

He turned to her. "I didn't know you could put a spoon in a pot to keep it from boiling over."

"You do now."

"Too bad you can't do that with human beings," he said.

"People don't boil," Anna said.

Mitch smiled. "That's what you think."

"I'm going to let that pass," she said.

"Good, because I'm starved. I don't have the energy for an argument."

"Cooking isn't as easy as you expected?" she asked.

"It's the temptations that can do you in."

"I'll let that pass, too," Anna said. "Now, if you'll open the wine, I'll get you something to relieve those temptations." Anna busied herself with setting out the dinnerware, napkins, and silver that Germaine had so kindly provided, then began opening the food containers they'd brought. While Mitch had struggled with the warm pasta salad, Anna had had time to prepare a sweet, crispy slaw and bake a chili-hot corn bread.

As soon as their plates were filled, and the wine was poured, Mitch began to eat. Anna watched with amazement at the amount of food he was putting away, and congratulated herself on packing enough. She'd thought she was overdoing it, but that wasn't the case at all.

"My God, this is good," Mitch said between bites.

"How can you tell?"

"I'll slow down in a minute," Mitch said good-humoredly. "Just let me get my strength back first."

"I didn't realize what a lot of energy it took to play the fiddle," she said, teasing.

Mitch smiled at her joking, but he remained silent. The lovemaking aside, it was the wear and tear on his psyche that had drained his reserves. He knew he had to gather his strength to begin the assault on her plans for the future, and the delicious food was just a start. He also knew that his timing should be perfect, but he doubted that an argument ever had a perfect time for beginning. His marriage to Betina had proven that fact of life very well.

"So, you like your own cooking?" Anna asked when Mitch had consumed more than two full plates.

"You think I can do this without your help?" he asked, pointing to the salad with his fork.

"Without a doubt. Cooking is like riding a bicycle. Once you get the basics, you can do it without thinking."

Mitch looked up from his plate. "But I don't want to do it without your help," he said seriously.

Anna's defenses were immediately on guard. "I'd call that a foul," Anna said.

Mitch knew exactly what she meant, but he decided to treat it lightly—for the moment. "Are we playing basketball?" he asked.

"We're not playing at anything, Mitch."

He shrugged. "It isn't against the rules to say what you feel, though. Right?"

Anna's own words came back to haunt her. "Guess I'm a little nervous," she said.

Mitch pushed his plate away. "Can't say as I blame you. You've made a risky decision. I'd be nervous, too, if I thought I had to bring up a child all by myself."

She could call interference, but calling a foul hadn't dissuaded him. Anna began gathering their picnic things to keep her hands busy and free her mind for thinking. Her insistence on noninterference should have been more clearly defined, but at the time she'd stated it, her goal hadn't been clear even to her. She had to admit that all that seemed to matter then had been having the child all to herself. Was it too late to elucidate further? she wondered. Could she now extend the meaning of nonintervention to include an attack on her decision as well?

"You're playing the devil's advocate," she said.

"You said we weren't playing at anything," he reminded her.

Anna gave him a half smile. "I'm either going to have to think things out more completely, or keep my mouth shut," she said.

"You're right about needing to think things out more completely," Mitch agreed and began helping her clean up the table.

"Meaning?" she asked.

"You told me you'd given this a lot of thought, but other than loving children and wanting a baby, you haven't told me why you don't want a husband, too."

"That should be obvious," she said tightly.

Mitch shook his head. "I'm afraid it isn't," he said.

"Exactly," she said. "You aren't even aware of your manipulating tactics, are you?"

"Manipulating tactics?" he asked angrily. But his outrage was short-lived. She was right; he'd had it in his mind to change her opinion from the very beginning.

"You're denying it?" she asked.

He closed the picnic basket and kept his eyes on the wooden cover. "No," he said softly.

"What right do you have to try to change my mind?" she asked bluntly.

"None. But you could be polite and listen to my opinion," he said.

Anna looked around her, then up at the children. Indecision clouded her mind, but, admittedly, Mitch was right. "I'll listen," she said finally.

"Let's go for a walk," he said, turning from the table and standing.

The picnic hamper safely in the trunk of the car, they began walking back toward where the children were playing. Neither spoke for a time, but Anna felt uncomfortable with the silence. The inevitable didn't get any more palatable with the delay.

"You were going to give me an opinion," she reminded him reluctantly.

"Maybe I shouldn't," he said. "You trusted me not to be judgmental."

"So what you have to say defines black and white?" she asked.

"Not exactly. It's a question."

"Then ask it."

"Don't you think kids are better off with two parents?" He said the words quickly, before he lost his nerve.

"No," she answered immediately.

"Tell me why."

"It isn't a simple answer. It's more like a collection of impressions. In a large family you get a taste of everything. My mother is repressed, my sister was controlled, and my aunt Theresa agreed to send her children away to boarding school against her will in exchange for keeping her marriage intact. My oldest brother has divorced two women. One couldn't cook well enough to suit him, and the other didn't keep his house as clean as he thought she should. Need I go on?"

"So there's been a lot of marital strife in your family. What has that to do with you?" Mitch asked.

"All the women I've told you about bought the Prince Charming dream, and they've paid a high price trying to live happily ever after. So much energy goes into keeping their husbands content that they have little left for anything else.''

"That's a pretty depressing picture you're painting.''

"And I'd like to avoid it.''

"All marriages aren't like that,'' he said.

"I know, but what are the odds? Have you been listening to the statistics? Barely a week goes by that some news program doesn't quote the numbers on divorce.''

"So you listened to the numbers and made up your mind, is that it?''

"That's one aspect of it, yes,'' she said.

"And you don't give any thought to whether your child will *need* two parents, right?''

"Donanne and George Thomas seem to be doing all right,'' she reminded him.

"You think they couldn't do better?'' he asked, frustrated almost to the point of anger.

"Since I didn't know G.T.'s father, I couldn't speak for him, but Donanne is a very happy child now.''

"Now that she doesn't have an interfering father,'' he said contemptuously.

"That's right,'' Anna said.

Mitch stopped walking in front of a wrought-iron bench and pointed toward the swings. "What about that father over there? Is he interfering?''

"How could I know? But look again. I'd say he's one out of thirty parents here with their children—twenty-nine women, one man."

Mitch sat down with a sigh. "Fathers have to work," he said defensively.

"That's what they say... But then what do they do with their free time? The ones I know don't play with their children."

"You have all the answers, don't you?" he said, looking up at her.

"When the questions are about what I think is best for me," she answered.

"But you're not the only one involved. Don't you think you should consider the child?"

Anna sat down beside him. "I am," she said.

"You are the most frustrating—"

"Hold it right there, Mr. McCabe. If I remember correctly, you said you admired the fact that I make my own rules and stick to them."

"And you said I was a very persuasive man," he reminded her. "You can't blame me for trying."

She turned and frowned at him. "I'm not sure *what* you're trying to do, Mitchell," she said honestly. "It may be a little late to change my mind about getting pregnant. And if that's what you're doing—"

"No!"

"You want to marry me," she said flatly.

"You could do worse."

"Not if I'm alone," she said with more conviction than she really felt.

Mitch leaned forward and pressed his hands against his knees. The deep breath didn't calm him, and he was at a loss for words. It seemed to be the time to retreat and regroup. The two-parent argument was at a standstill.

"Is that it?" Anna asked, and she hoped that it was. Her determination had started to erode hours ago, but she didn't want him to know it. Something in her head was driving the conviction home, while her heart just kept on trying to outsmart her.

"For now," he said.

Their argument and the feelings of frustration it had caused had been left behind in the park. Neither was anxious to jeopardize the mutual friendship they'd started to build. Anna began to feel a sense of urgency. Unmistakably, the pregnancy she wished for made her time with Mitch all the more important, but a growing restlessness was beginning to invade. Against her will, Mitch was becoming the most delightful part of her life.

"You haven't tried to change my mind for days," Anna said and snuggled a little closer.

"Disappointed?" Mitch asked with a smile.

Anna touched his nose with a finger. "Just curious, cowboy," she said lightly. "And maybe a little bit grateful." But she wasn't really grateful. She'd brought up the subject because she'd actually missed his hinting at the possibility of a life together.

Mitch lay back on the pillows and crossed his arms behind his head. In the past several days, it had taken great restraint to keep from continuing his assault. The hours they'd been together when neither was working had been spent making love and little else. Even then, he'd wanted to be with her every other minute of every day that passed.

He'd spent so much time evaluating and questioning his own motives for doing what he was doing that he'd almost been able to discount Anna's. He was certain that it was just a matter of time until he could come up with the perfect plan. He wanted to spend a lifetime with her and nothing else mattered.

"Did you hear that?" Anna asked.

"What?"

"Knocking. I think someone is at your bedroom door."

Mitch listened. "You're right. Be right back."

Anna watched as he pulled on the dark blue robe she'd bought him for their one-week anniversary. He was such a gorgeous man that every time she looked at him she was in danger of losing control. In the past few days, she'd become almost unrecognizable to herself as far as deportment was concerned. When she was with him, her appetite for having him near was insatiable. She missed him even now, and he was only in the next room.

In a few moments he returned. "Got a phone call downstairs," he said.

"At this time of the morning?"

"Probably my Uncle Thomas. Farmers don't pay attention to the clock. Be back in a minute." He turned and grinned when he reached the doorway. "Don't forget where we were."

"Not a chance," Anna said.

"Hey, old buddy! How's it goin'?"

"Joey?" Mitch asked.

"'Course it's Joey. Who'd ya think?"

"Where are you?" Mitch asked.

"Well, now, that's the thing…"

Uh-oh. *Here it comes,* Mitch thought.

"I'm over here in the Huber Creek hospital, old buddy," Joey said.

"Are you all right? What happened?"

"Seems like Old Blue was feelin' kinda cantankerous last night…didn't think he needed to be put up. Kicked the hellfire out of my leg, he did."

"Is it broken?" Mitch took a breath. "Of course it's broken! Hey, I'm sorry, Joey."

"I'm the one's sorry there, Mitch. Vacation's shot to hell. Leg's shot to hell. One thing, though."

"What's that?"

"Old Blue's just fine," Joey said.

Mitch had been so busy worrying about Joey that

he'd forgotten about the horses. "That's good to hear...but who's out there now?" he asked.

"You won't go gettin' upset?" Joey asked.

Mitch was immediately on guard. "I won't get upset," he said cautiously.

"It's kind of a roundabout story how it happened, see. The doctor asked me if he should call anyone, and I said I had a sister over in Kermit. Well, he says he'd better call her and tell her what happened just in case I had any business I had to take care of. Guess I was pretty groggy 'bout then. Well, I said I had some horses to look after, and he says maybe she could find someone to do it for me."

"Joey, can you get to the point? Is there somebody out there with the stock or not?"

"I'm gettin' to it, just keep your pants on," Joey said impatiently. "Anyhow, Betina came on over last night, and she said she's been tryin' to get out to your place for the past two weeks...said some cuss from down Dimmit County wants to have a look at Old Blue for stud. Wantin' to start up a line or somethin'."

"Are you telling me that Betina is taking care of my horses?"

"Not likely, old buddy. You know how she feels about critters. But this Dimmit County fella said he'd stick around till I got hold of you. Said he was lookin' for some property around here anyway, and Betina'd been showin' him what's for sale."

"Cabe Corner isn't for sale, Joey," Mitch said.

"'Course it isn't. But you know Betina."

"I sure do," Mitch said. "Tell her I'll be there by noon." *And I'll get there before that if I know what's good for me,* he thought. "You gonna be all right, Joey?" Mitch asked.

"I'm gonna be fine," Joey said.

"Okay to call Don in to play?" Mitch asked.

"He'll be glad to get the work, Mitch."

"Good. Then I'll see you later today, okay?"

"Sure thing, good buddy. Hey, Mitch?"

"Yeah?"

"Betina's lookin' real good."

"She always did, Joey."

"Yeah, but—"

"See you later, Joey." Mitch hung up the phone and hit the wall with his fist. "Damn!"

"Hey, take it easy there, nephew. This old house is a hundred years old."

"Sorry," Mitch said.

"Well?"

Mitch knew that "well" was his cue; he told Germaine what had happened. "And if that's not bad enough," he went on, "I wanted to take Anna down to see Uncle Thomas."

"So take her when you get back," Germaine suggested.

Mitch frowned. "She works, I work. We have all

of four more days off before she goes back to San Antonio.''

"Sounds serious," Germaine said, smiling.

Mitch realized, too late, he'd given his feelings away. "Not *that* serious," he said lightly. At least he didn't feel that he'd violated their agreement in any way.

"Suit yourself," Germaine said.

"I'll work it out," Mitch said.

"I'm sure you will, Mitchell."

By the time he'd gotten Don on the phone, called the airport to charter a plane, and made all the other necessary arrangements, he *did* have it worked out. He'd take Anna with him. No problem. Once they got there, he'd get Forrest and his son to take turns feeding, and Drex could stay the weekends. Everything could be taken care of in twenty-four hours, and that would still leave him some time to show Anna around the place.

Well, one problem—if Anna knew where they were going, she'd be certain he was trying to influence her in some way. The oil wells had turned more than one pretty head, and she'd be thinking he was trying to turn hers with money. Then there was the little matter of Betina's being there.

He stopped at the top of the stairs and looked down. He'd rather take a head-first tumble all the way to the bottom than leave Anna for any longer than he had to. He rubbed his fingers across his chin and realized he needed a shave. He needed to shower and dress. She'd need to do the same plus pack a change of clothes. How could he get her to do that? he wondered.

Who'd said it? Somebody had said it, and that was good enough: "All's fair in love and war." And this was love!

"Thought we might go down to my uncle's place today. Okay with you?" Mitch asked casually when he came back into the room.

"Is everything all right, Mitch? The call wasn't bad news or—"

"No. No, everything's fine. Why?"

"You look a little worried."

"Hey, I was just getting lonesome down there."

"Then just come over here and I'll keep you company for a while," she said suggestively.

"Well..."

"Well, what?" Anna asked.

"We're kind of expected," he said, then knew he shouldn't have.

Just like a man, Anna thought, making plans and telling you later. "Why don't you go on? I have some shopping to do anyway." That wasn't quite the truth. While Mitch had been gone, she'd begun to feel a bit queasy.

"I didn't mean that the way it sounded," he said. "We talked about going a couple of days ago, and I thought we'd agreed. It's a nice drive in the morning, and anyway—''

"Come here," Anna interrupted.

Mitch sat down on the edge of the bed, ready, but not looking forward to a lecture about male manipulative tactics.

"I can be ready in twenty minutes," Anna said, smiling.

"My uncle is looking forward to meeting—" His argument halted. "Twenty minutes?"

"Maybe less, but I want to take a shower."

Mitch grinned. "Need some help?"

"An interesting proposition. How are you at scrubbing backs?"

"Let's make that an hour," Mitch said, as he began to pull the quilts slowly away from her naked body.

One hour later they were in the car.

"Got your toothbrush and a change of clothes in case of fog?" Mitch asked, hoping she didn't notice that they were going in the wrong direction.

"I brought everything you told me to," she said. And a few crackers to quell the upset stomach, she added silently. "You think we'll be staying the night?"

"Never can tell."

"I'm anxious to meet your aunt and uncle. Germaine's told me a lot about them."

"Fine people," Mitch said.

"Is it a long drive?" Anna asked, beginning to feel the threat of nausea again, but overjoyed at its significance.

"Not much longer," he said.

"This doesn't look like what I imagined the delta would look like," she commented casually.

"Well, I have a stop to make first."

"What kind of stop?"

"It's kind of a surprise," he said.

Anna turned on him. "Mitchell McCabe—"

"Hold on now." He turned the car into a fenced enclosure and the man at the gate waved at him with a friendly smile.

"Morning, Mr. McCabe," the man said as Mitch slowed to a stop.

"Sandy ready?" Mitch asked.

"And waiting, sir," the man said. "You're a little later than you said you'd be."

Mitch glanced at Anna. "Business," he said to the man. "Couldn't be helped." When he looked back at Anna she was blushing beautifully.

He slowly pulled through the gate. "I enjoyed your shower, too," he said. "Maybe we could make it a habit."

"You're quite impossible, you know, Mr. McCabe."

"And you're quite beautiful, Miss Harte," he said, as he pulled into a parking place beside a larger hangar.

"Will you be long?" Anna asked as Mitch opened his door.

"Come with me. Maybe you can hurry things along."

Mitch approached a red-haired man and spoke to him briefly, while Anna got out of the car. He seemed nervous. "You said something about a surprise?" she reminded him when he came around the car.

"Right this way, madam." He crooked his arm, and she looped her hand through it. "A brief tour," he said, then looked away from her so the lie wouldn't show.

Eight

"Well, what do you think of her?" Mitch asked when they were inside the aircraft.

Anna turned all the way around, then rubbed her hand over the plush blue covering on the back of one of the six seats in the cabin. "It's just beautiful, Mitch."

"Come back here," he said and motioned to her. "It's called a refreshment cabinet."

"Mmm, coffee smells good," Anna said. "This is really wonderful."

"Mr. William Lear's last design before he died," Mitch said. "You like her?"

"Of course."

"Good, because I'm thinking about buying her."

"Well, congratulations, but you don't need my approval for that."

"Just thought you might like to see her," Mitch said, "and maybe take a test flight," he added casually.

Anna eyed him suspiciously. "I thought your Uncle Thomas was expecting us."

Mitch put on his most innocent face. "A little white lie to keep the surprise a secret. Forgive me?"

Anna put her hands behind his neck and locked his eyes with hers. "You are a born strategist, Mitchell McCabe, and you're not going to stop maneuvering, are you?" she said in her sternest tone.

"Surprises don't count, do they?" Mitch asked.

"It's one coup after another, isn't it?"

He smiled. "You have to be cunning to survive—*and* to surprise," he said.

"Well, I approve of this one," she said, finally returning his smile.

Mitch let out the breath he'd been holding. "Then let's sit down and enjoy," he said.

Sandy was already at the controls. His entrance into the plane had gone unnoticed by Anna, but she wasn't surprised. She'd been rather well occupied by an expert tactician. They waited only moments on the taxi ramp, then were airborne shortly after lining up on the runway. Lake Pontchartrain soon disappeared from sight on their starboard side, the early morning fog quickly hiding the surface detail from view.

Anna could barely hear the pilot as he spoke to the tower. She settled back in her seat and watched as the powerful jet engines lifted them through the fog and low cloud cover into clear blue sky. When they leveled out, she was aware of Mitch's movement, but paid no attention to what he was doing. In a few moments, he was beside her seat, lowering the table in front of her, and placing a tray on it. She glanced at the tray, then looked up at him, surprised.

"This should tide you over till lunch," he said.

"You're just full of interesting tricks today."

"And every other day if I can manage it," he said, pleased with her reaction.

"Just keep them pleasant ones, like this," she warned.

"I'll try," he said evasively.

Mitch brought a tray for himself and sat down again. She'd been wrong when she'd said that people didn't boil, he thought. He was sure that the churning in his gut couldn't be anything less. The delicious French pastry he'd had Sandy pick up on the way to the airport felt like a knot in his stomach. He'd decided that Lake Charles, not quite two hundred miles into the trip, would be the longest he could delay telling her where they were going.

A glance at his watch told him they'd been airborne about thirty minutes. The moment of truth was at hand. Stalling, he left his seat, returned their trays to the galley, then poured himself fresh coffee. Strangely, Anna hadn't touched hers.

"How do you like it so far?" he asked when he sat back down.

"I've never been in a small jet like this," she said. "It's really nice, Mitch."

"I think so, too."

"If you're thinking about buying it, shouldn't you be up front with the pilot getting the feel of it?" she asked.

"I'd rather be back here with you," he said.

"That's very sweet, but—"

"Hold that thought for a minute," he interrupted.

"What thought?" she asked.

"About how sweet I am."

"All right," she said warily.

"There's just one more little part to this surprise— maybe the best part of all," he said cheerfully.

How bad could it be? Why not let him have his fun? she thought. "What is it?" she asked.

"We're going to Cabe Corner."

It took a moment for the information to sink in, but when she realized what he'd said, she couldn't believe it. "We're going to your home?" she asked, her voice pounding the words across the narrow space between them.

"Just for the night," he assured her. "I'm not kidnapping you." He paused. "But maybe that wouldn't be such a bad idea, either."

Anna sank back in her seat. "This is unreal," she said, surprised.

"A little unexpected, perhaps, but not unreal," he said.

She turned on him. "Why the deceit? Why all the secrecy? Why couldn't you just ask me to go with you like any other civilized person?"

Mitch had been ready for her outburst. "You might have said no," he answered simply.

"And that would have been some kind of disaster?" she asked caustically.

"I had to make the trip, and I didn't want to go without you. If I'd insisted..." He shrugged.

"I still don't understand why you couldn't have just asked me—wait a minute! You're not telling me *all* the truth yet, are you?"

"The important parts," he said.

"I don't like this one bit, Mitchell McCabe." She turned away from him. "And I was foolish enough to compliment you this morning on not trying to change my mind over the last few days."

"Try to see this from my point of view," he suggested.

She faced him again, glaring. "Oh, believe me, I can," she said. "You thought if I could see your lovely home and all your beautiful oil wells, I'd be so impressed that I'd change my mind about everything." She pointed at him. "Don't think for one minute I don't know what you're doing. You're just like all the rest."

Mitch captured her hand and held it. "No, I'm not like all the rest," he said quietly. "I'm the only father your child is going to have."

Anna struggled with her ambivalence and felt like crying. If she'd known from the beginning how inextricably their lives would become entwined, she might not have told him about wanting a baby at all. At least she'd have been able to make a more rational decision, though she couldn't imagine what it might have been. She would most certainly have given each of them more time to think and talk through the possible outcome. How could she have known that any man would want to marry "Aunt Anna," Miss Prim and Proper Anna, the spinster of the Harte family? she wondered.

But she wasn't Miss Prim and Proper Anna anymore, she admitted reluctantly. Aunt Anna was hardly recognizable anymore, at least on the inside. She hadn't had the nerve to wear it yet, but she'd even bought a low-necked, red satin nightgown. It was in her overnight case at this very moment. Her dream hadn't changed, but she had to take part of the blame for his, she realized. Still, that didn't make his deceitful ways any more acceptable.

At the very least, she owed him empathy. Second thoughts had plagued her from their first night together, and her own uncertainty had probably misled him. It was still confusing her—and she was afraid.

Her fear explained her overreaction to his pressuring, and the fear was real. It had molded her impressions into fast and firm decisions about her own future. Charleen's and Donanne's unhappiness seemed always on her mind. Jerry Hayford was certainly Donanne's only father, but that didn't make him the right man for either his wife or his daughter. If only she hadn't pressured her father into sending her to New Orleans to apprentice with Pep, she thought, but that had been her choice, too.

"This is about control, Mitch," she said finally. "I feel as if I'll lose myself if I continue to live for others. I wish you could understand."

"That's very difficult for me," he said.

"Then you've never allowed someone else to determine the circumstances of your life."

"That's true," he said.

"I know I have the right to choose my own lifestyle, even if my choice isn't compatible with anyone else's."

"That's true, too," he agreed.

"I don't have any desire to control *you*," she said.

"So the harder I try, the further behind I get, right?"

"Behind what?" she asked.

"Your eight ball."

Anna had to smile.

"I wish I'd been better prepared for you, Anna Harte," he said.

"What do you mean?"

"Most of the women I've known have wanted to be controlled...maybe 'guided' is a better word," he amended.

"Maybe they were waiting for someone wonderful to take charge," she said. "That's the Prince Charming myth I was talking about."

"I don't ride a white horse," he said with half a smile on his face.

Anna spread her hands and lifted them, palms up. "What do you call this?" she asked, looking about the cabin.

"Guess that's a 'gotcha,'" he said. "But I'm not sorry you're here."

"To be completely truthful, I'm not either," she said.

"You still disapprove of my tactics, though."

"It doesn't really matter. You have the same rights that I do, so I don't have to approve," she said.

Mitch kept silent. There was enough danger lurking already, especially with the probability of Betina's presence at Cabe Corner. He had no idea how Anna would react to his ex-wife, but he would find out soon enough. He'd taken risks before, and he suspected that this was probably the most foolish of his thirty-six years.

* * *

The landing at the county airport was a smooth one, and the two-hour flight had passed so quickly that Anna was surprised when they touched down. She decided that she might have been dozing lightly for the past half-hour or so, and she had trouble finding a logical reason for her relaxed state. When she became fully aware of her surroundings, she realized that Mitch had taken her still full coffee cup away, raised her table, and covered her with a light blanket.

"Thank you," she said softly as she looked over at him.

"Too many irons in the fire, I guess," he said.

"Just enough," she said, and she placed her hands protectively over her abdomen.

"Shall we go?" he asked.

"You're the boss," she said, lifting the blanket and handing it to him.

Mitch let it go even though her tone had been neither sarcastic nor derogatory, and they were soon leaving the airport in the four-wheel drive he'd left there.

Living in the city all her life hadn't prepared Anna for the vast spaces in the western part of her own home state. Through the dry clear air, the sky was bluer than she'd ever seen it. Unlike the area in the moister climate around San Antonio, the land seemed arid, the vegetation sparse, but it had a special quiet beauty that was especially soothing. They'd been driving only a short time when Mitch turned onto a side road and crossed an old, single-lane bridge that spanned a barely trickling stream.

"Huber Creek," he said. "The eastern boundary of Cabe Corner."

"So we're entering that little piece of heaven you told me about?"

"That's right. Used to be called Right's Creek, but an old test pilot totaled a Cessna in the middle of her one day and walked away from it. They changed the name for good luck. That was back in the, oh, late forties, early fifties, I guess."

"I see you've had pretty good luck here," Anna said, looking out through the windshield at two tirelessly pumping oil wells.

"Thanks to old Huber, probably," he said.

They turned south just over the bridge and followed the creek and a white-painted fence until a large stand of trees came into view. The trees looked as if they'd been misplaced from some wetter clime, and they stood out against the blue sky like an oasis in the rugged country that surrounded them. A low, white frame structure sat half hidden in the tree-filtered, noon sunlight. The gravel road turned sharply right, as did the creek beside it, and became a driveway, ending in a large, shaded circle where two other cars were parked.

"Used to be an old barn, back in the thirties," Mitch said, pointing to the house. "The original homestead sat on that little hill we passed half a mile back. Tornado flattened it about twenty years ago, so they moved down here and started adding on.''

"I didn't expect Cabe Corner to look so homey," Anna said.

"Just one surprise after another," Mitch said lightly.

"But where are the horses?"

"The pastures go back to the west, beyond the house and trees. You can't see them from here, but I'll give you the tour later."

From the driveway, very little could be seen but the creek on the left and the L-shaped house to the right and straight ahead. In order to keep it under the trees, the house had been added onto at a right angle to the original structure. The setting gave Anna a feeling of cozy isolation from the sprawling arid land that surrounded it.

Her hand closed over the door handle, but she didn't begin the downward motion to open it. The front door of the house opened, and a striking woman, dressed in an immaculate white pantsuit, came hurrying toward them. She was around the vehicle and throwing herself into Mitch's arms before Anna could move. She planted a firm kiss on his lips, then held him tightly to her.

"God, you look good, Mitch!" she said exuberantly. "I've missed you. You can't imagine how much."

Mitch cleared his throat. "Hello, Betina." He

gently pried her arms from around his neck, but she held on to his hands. "I want you to meet someone," he said.

Betina turned her head, looked briefly in Anna's direction, then returned her gaze to Mitch. "It's so good to have you home," she said, making it sound as if the home still belonged to them both, and he'd just taken a short business trip.

"Thanks for taking care of things," Mitch said, his voice strained.

"You know I was more than glad to do it," she cooed. "For you, I'd do just about anything."

"Uh-huh," Mitch agreed. "So let me introduce you to a friend of mine, okay?"

"Of course, hon. Introduce away."

The two of them came around to Anna's door, and Mitch opened it. Standing up in front of the taller Betina gave Anna the very uncomfortable sense of being overpowered. The woman wore her long, abundant, unnaturally red hair in a striking style swept back from her face. Her skin was porcelain white and flawless, and her makeup looked professionally done.

Against the brilliant white of her blouse, many strands of fine gold chain stood out like the streaks of sunlight that shone through the new spring leaves on the trees. No less than four diamond and gold rings adorned perfectly manicured hands.

"This is Anna Harte," Mitch said.

"So nice to meet you, dear," Betina said in a condescending tone, then turned to Mitch. "I'm sure she'll be comfortable in the guest room. I aired out the whole house and brought in a few groceries." She glanced in Anna's direction. "Hope I brought enough. I wasn't expecting a guest."

That's obvious, Anna thought, and wished she could get back in the wagon and drive all the way to New Orleans.

"There'll be enough," Mitch said shortly. He reached for Anna's hand.

Anna moved away from him as if she hadn't seen his gesture and went to the rear of the wagon. Extracting her small overnight case from the luggage space gave her some small satisfaction. She wanted Betina to know, without a doubt, that she would be staying the night. Why she cared was a puzzle, but she didn't try to solve it. The important thing seemed to be to clarify her relationship with Mitch. For the time being, she was a special person in his life, and she wanted Betina to know it.

Mitch was by her side, taking the case from her and pulling out his own small shaving kit. He started for the front door, and Betina lost no time in catching up with him and putting a possessive arm about his waist. Her manner was bouncy and vigorous, her look of satisfaction a particularly irritating note of dissonance in the quiet afternoon.

As soon as they were inside, Betina took Anna's suitcase from him. "I'll put this in the guest room," she said, and she was walking rapidly away before Mitch could say anything.

He turned to Anna. "Let her go for now. She'll be out of here before the sun goes down."

"I wouldn't bet on that," Anna said flatly.

"She doesn't live here," Mitch said.

"I couldn't have guessed it," Anna said.

"I should have explained why she's here, but we…well, we were talking about other things and…"

"You don't have to explain."

"But I intend to. I'll put some water on for tea, and I'll tell you everything. Deal?"

"I'd like to wash up," Anna said. "Just point the way to the guest room, all right?" She put special emphasis on "guest room," but the jab at his conscience didn't make her feel any better.

He pointed to his right. "Down that hall, last door on the right. I'll be in the kitchen over there." He pointed to his left.

She was disappointed that he'd obliged her so quickly. Perhaps she would be exiled to the guest room for the duration. She passed a smiling Betina in the hallway, found the room without trouble, and closed the door behind her. It felt good to be alone, away from the irritating cheerfulness of the other woman. But as she washed her hands and combed her hair, she found that she was impatient to get back and insert her presence between Mitch and his glamorous ex-wife.

Use a little restraint, she told herself, then crossed to the corner windows. She was in the room that formed the right angle of the house, and she could see both to the north and the west. Between the trees there was not a horse in sight, but the gleaming white fences continued and formed a quilting pattern outlining fields of spring-green grass.

The effect was startling. Out the north windows, the dry land rose in amber beauty to underline the pristine blue of the sky, while through the west windows the living vegetation followed the creek for as far as the eye could see. The land was like its owner, both rugged and vital, strong for survival, while gentle for nurturing.

Anna sat down in one of the chairs in the windowed corner, suddenly weak with revelation. Her objection to the ways of men had never interfered with her love for them. She truly loved her father as well as her brothers and uncles. All seemed to fit her concept of the typical male, but the flaw she perceived had not influenced her affection; it had only structured the vision of her future.

She had never integrated her feelings into rational thought and words. She'd existed very comfortably with the seemingly contradictory concepts, but she had not ever wondered why it was possible. Her jealousy of Betina contradicted the future vision. If she didn't want him, why envy the woman who did? The rivalry was irrational.

Anna left the chair and opened the case that Betina had left on the bed. She put her makeup in the bathroom and her clothes in the empty top drawer of the dresser, then slid the suitcase under the bed. Satisfied with her decision to stay in the guest room, she entered the hall with a feeling of renewed conviction. She had power over her life, and every step, however small, in the direction of sovereignty was a move in the right direction.

As she approached the kitchen door, she heard a loud pop. She entered to find Betina alone and holding a bottle of champagne. Two tulip-shaped goblets sat on the counter near the sink. Anna smiled to herself. The woman was performing acts of seduction that would never have entered Anna's mind. The effect was one of almost smug satisfaction on Anna's part.

The water was boiling for tea, and Anna crossed directly to it, filling the teapot. "Excuse me, where are the cups?" she asked sweetly.

Betina lost no time in reaching into a cabinet, extracting a heavy mug, and handing it to Anna.

"I'd prefer a cup if you have one," Anna said.

Betina frowned, went back into the same cabinet, and pulled a cup and saucer from its interior. "Will this do?" she asked.

"It's fine, thank you."

"Mmm, smells good," Mitch said as he came back into the room.

Anna poured tea into the cup Betina had given her and handed it to Mitch, then got herself another. Her hand was poised on the handle of the pot when Mitch noticed the champagne.

"What's this?" he asked lightly.

"I feel like celebrating every time you come home," Betina said. It sounded as if she'd been there each time it had happened.

Maybe she had, Anna thought, but she refused to be provoked.

"I think that's a good idea," Mitch said. Without a word, he went to the cabinet and brought out another goblet. "I'll pour," he said, taking the bottle from Betina.

Her face might have been in danger of cracking if the smile she felt in her heart had been transferred to it. Anna accepted the glass Mitch offered, then sat down in the chair he pulled out from the table in the center of the kitchen.

"I propose a toast," Mitch said when all three of them were seated. "To the comfort of my guest while she stays here."

Reluctantly, Betina touched the glass to her lips, but she didn't drink. She seemed about to propose a toast of her own, but Mitch began talking.

"Now, tell me about Joey," he said to Betina. "Is he all right?"

"Joey's fine," she said shortly.

"Anna and I will visit him later this afternoon,"

Mitch said, then turned to Anna. "Old Blue gave Joey a pretty good kick last night," he explained. "He's in the hospital with a broken leg. That's who called me this morning."

"Oh, my." Anna looked at Betina, and her contempt dissolved into concern. "You must be very worried about your brother."

Betina glanced at Mitch, the look of surprise plain on her face. "Yes," she said hesitantly.

"What can I do to help?" Anna asked Mitch, her already waning anger over being "kidnapped" completely forgotten.

"You can keep me company while I straighten things out," he said. "We'll have to visit a couple of people and ask for their help."

"You could just call them," Betina suggested.

"Forrest is hardly ever near the phone. He spends his time outside with his stock or working in that garden of his. His son is in school. No, we'll have to go find him."

"Suit yourself," Betina said.

"Has Drex been by since you got here?" Mitch asked Betina.

"He's out with Mr. Cambridge right now," Betina said.

"Mr. Cambridge?" Mitch asked.

"A client of mine," Betina said.

"The man Joey told me about…wants to look at Old Blue, right?"

"Among other things," Betina said.

"I understand he took care of the horses this morning. If I don't see him before you two leave, you'll thank him for me, won't you?"

Betina hesitated. "He won't be leaving before he has a chance to talk to you," she said.

"All right." Mitch finished his wine and stood up. "I'm going to call the hospital. Then I guess it's time we got started," he said to Anna.

"I'm ready whenever you are," Anna said.

Mitch turned to Betina. "I know you must be wanting to get back to your business," he said. "But would you mind staying here until Drex gets back? I want you to tell him to wait for me."

"I'll stay," Betina said grudgingly.

"Good. Be right back."

Mitch left the room, and Betina reached for the champagne bottle. She poured her glass full, then put the bottle down without offering any to Anna. It didn't matter; Anna had only taken one sip anyway. Betina inspected the manicure of her left hand, then twisted at the large diamond on her ring finger with her thumb.

"That's a beautiful ring," Anna said conversationally.

"Mitch gave it to me," Betina said.

"He has excellent taste," Anna said.

Betina glared at Anna. "I question his taste in some

things,'' she said, obviously referring to the women in his life in general, and to Anna in particular.

''I understand you're very successful in your real estate business,'' Anna said, actually enjoying Betina's discomfort.

''I get by,'' Betina said sullenly.

Anna made a point of looking at the other three expensive rings the woman wore. ''I guess real estate has its up and downs just like everything else.''

''Like relationships,'' Betina said. ''And my relationship with Mitch is on its way up.''

''I'm glad to hear it,'' Anna said easily.

Betina looked at her, surprised. Then she frowned. ''Don't kid with me, honey. I can spot a gold digger a mile away.''

''That doesn't surprise me,'' Anna said sweetly.

''I want you to know that I'm not going to tolerate any interference here,'' Betina said sternly.

''You won't have to worry about any from me.''

''You're saying you don't want him?'' Betina asked.

''That's right,'' Anna said.

''Then just stay the hell out of my way, lady, 'cause I'm holding a handful of aces.''

Nine

There was a chill in the spring evening air by the time they returned to Cabe Corner, and Mitch got a fire started in the living room before he went out to take care of the horses. There was no one in the house, but Mitch didn't comment on Betina's absence, probably because her car was still in the driveway. Anna volunteered to help him with his chores, but he insisted that she stay inside where it was warm.

"Promise I'll get that tour tomorrow morning?" she asked.

"That's a promise," he assured her.

"You won't mind if I poke around the kitchen while you're gone, will you?"

"Just make yourself at home. I won't be long," he said, moving toward the front door.

"Think I'll see what I can put together for dinner," she said.

"Now, that sounds like a real winner. It'll be the first time that kitchen's seen a real cook since I moved in."

"Didn't Betina cook?" she asked.

Mitch lifted a cowboy hat off a rack near the door and put it on. "Not on a bet, she didn't," he said as he stepped outside.

Anna wasn't surprised, but instead of gloating, she simply felt sorry for Mitch. She was glad that over the past two weeks she'd been able to show him how to prepare a few simple recipes. For the first time since their arrival, Anna had a chance to look around, and she was able to take a moment to absorb the feeling of her surroundings.

Mitch had lived alone here for the past five years, and Anna was pleasantly surprised that the old converted barn looked more like a home than the bachelor's pad she had envisioned. Barn siding, brick, and the wide fireplace lent a rustic spirit to the north wall of the living room and extended to the original old barn door, which was still in place on the north wall of the dining room.

A combination of odd furniture pieces and the weathered wood of the support and ceiling beams created a cozy, informal atmosphere in which Anna felt relaxed. The entire effect was one of comfort, a place where people could abandon their coats and ties and cares. The kitchen had the same effect: a many-windowed sanctuary that was both modernly convenient, with built-in stovetop and many appliances, while still keeping in touch with the rugged beauty of the old structure.

Betina had been right about bringing in just a "few" groceries. There were two large steaks, two baking potatoes, two tomatoes, butter, sour cream, a dozen eggs, a small wedge of cheese, and several bottles of wine. An inventory of the kitchen cabinets provided a few staples, flour, an onion that had begun to sprout, canned goods, and a few spices.

Anna assembled the ingredients in her mind, then set to work. In a short time she'd transformed the flour into a thin batter and had a stack of light crêpes cooked and on a covered plate in the oven to keep warm. She sliced the steak into thin strips, diced the onion, quickly sautéed both in butter, then fashioned a sauce from sour cream, canned asparagus, and a sprinkling of wine and spices.

While the potatoes cooked in the microwave, Anna sat down at the kitchen table. She considered the inner peace she was feeling. In spite of Betina's presence and the woman's vindictive manner, Anna was happy. She placed a hand over her flat stomach. Amazing how such a tiny little thing could turn the world around, she thought. She'd felt good all afternoon.

They'd found Joey Costella in high spirits when they'd visited his hospital room, and Anna could tell that Mitch was very relieved to see his friend in such good shape. His relief had been short-lived, however, when Joey began to talk about his nephew. Mitch had never told Anna about Betina's two-year-old son, the product of her second marriage, which had lasted only a year and a half.

Anna had felt that Joey was trying to draw Mitch into the triangle in some way, insinuating that Mitch should take some responsibility for Betina's parental tasks, though he never came right out and said it in plain English. Mitch had been obviously uncomfortable with the conversation, and he had tried time and again to change the subject.

She had found herself actually envious of Betina, wishing that the child for whom she waited were already here, already comfortable in her arms. The thought excited her anew as she stood, then crossed to the stove to tend the sauce. A sudden feeling of dizziness stopped her from lifting the lid, and she leaned heavily against the counter until the brief light-headedness had passed.

Instead of being frightened, she was thrilled, and thoroughly convinced that the strange phenomenon was yet another harbinger of good news. She rarely felt ill, and the intrusion of both nausea and vertigo on her robust health and plentiful energy surely meant that her pregnancy was no longer just a dream. Anna straightened from the cabinet, took a deep breath, then went about her dinner preparations with a renewed sense of vigor and well-being.

She'd finished mashing the potatoes and stuffing the four half shells, adding a little of the diced onion and grated cheese. She was tossing tomato wedges, black olives, and canned, whole green beans with some vinegar, oil, and pepper when she heard the front door slam to the accompaniment of several loud and angry voices. Betina's strident tones were especially vehement and easily heard.

"The price is much more than fair," Anna heard Betina say.

"The price is ridiculously high," Mitch countered.

"Mr. Cambridge wouldn't have offered it if he'd thought it was ridiculous. Would you, Mr. Cambridge?" she asked.

"That's right," a man's voice said.

"I'm going to say this just one more time, Betina. Cabe Corner is not for sale. Not at any price," Mitch said.

Anna heard the clink of glasses and knew that someone had gone behind the bar in the living room and was pouring drinks.

"Scotch, Mr. Cambridge?" Betina asked.

"Fine," he said.

"Nothing," Mitch said.

"Now that's a good boy," Betina said sweetly. "It's better you stay sober for this anyway."

"I don't need to be sober to say *no* to this contract of yours, Betina. It's a farce," Mitch said, and Anna heard the swish of papers being thrown aside.

"I don't think you get the whole picture, Mitch," Betina said.

Anna cringed at Betina's threatening tone, and she was starting to feel guilty about listening to the conversation going on in the other room. She put the tomatoes and green beans in the refrigerator, then went into the dining room fully intending to announce her presence to all.

"One way or another, you're going to say yes to me," Betina said. "Whether you like it or not, you have to take care of your responsibilities, both to me and to little Jess. You owe—"

"Stop right there, Betina," Mitch interrupted her angrily.

Anna moved quickly forward into the living room before Mitch could continue. Not only did she not want to hear what he was about to say, but she also didn't want them to think she'd been eavesdropping. Mitch immediately left his position by the fireplace and came to her. Neither Betina nor Mr. Cambridge made a move from their chairs, but both looked in her direction.

"Come sit down," Mitch said, as he put his arm around her waist. "Mr. Cambridge, this is Anna Harte."

The thin, blond man made a move to stand, but

Anna held her hand up. "Please don't get up. Glad to meet you, Mr. Cambridge."

"Same, I'm sure," he said, then lowered himself back into the chair with a sigh.

Anna took a few steps, then saw Betina's frown. "Mitch, I think I'd rather go to my room for a few minutes." Betina's frown changed into a victorious half smile.

"Are you all right?" Mitch asked.

"I'm fine, but I don't want to interfere with your business here."

"I have no business with these people." He looked at the other man. "Unless Mr. Cambridge wants to discuss stud fees again."

"I think we've pretty well settled all that," Mr. Cambridge said.

"But there's still a lot that *isn't* settled, Mitchell," Betina reminded him.

"It is, as far as I'm concerned," Mitch said.

"I have dinner ready," Anna said. "Why don't I set the table and—"

"Dinner for four?" Betina asked, obviously incredulous.

"Or five. I thought Drex might be staying," Anna said, relishing Betina's disbelief.

"Set the table, honey," Betina said to Anna. Then to Mr. Cambridge, she said. "This I've got to see."

"I'll help you," Mitch said to Anna.

"No, thanks, I don't need any help."

"I insist," Mitch said.

For the first time, Anna could appreciate his forceful manner and was glad that he preferred to be with her. "You might be useful at that," Anna said with a smile. "You know how to use a corkscrew, I presume?"

"You presume correctly, my good lady," Mitch said.

"Then we should be out of the kitchen in no time."

Anna heard a soft exclamatory sound from Betina as they left the room. She knew that the meal she'd prepared would be perfectly delicious, and she couldn't wait to observe the other woman's reaction. While Mitch opened the wine and carried dishes to the dining room table, Anna filled the delicate crêpes with the savory, sauced beef, and arranged three on each of the four dinner plates she'd had warming in the oven. The stuffed potatoes and tomato salad completed the attractive arrangement of food.

Mitch poured a hearty Burgundy into their wineglasses, as Anna brought the plates to the table. As an extra touch of elegance, Anna transferred a short, chubby candle in a pottery holder from the buffet to the center of the table and lit it.

"That should do it," she said.

"In a most spectacular way," Mitch said softly, the pride in her accomplishments showing plainly on his face.

"Dinner's ready," Anna said, as she stepped into the living room.

When Betina saw the table, her animated conversation with Mr. Cambridge ceased abruptly. "I see you two visited more than the hospital this afternoon," she said. "I didn't know the grocery was open that late in Huber Creek."

"It isn't," Mitch said, smiling.

"But all this..."

"I'm afraid I just had to make do with what you brought, Betina," Anna said. "Thank you for being so thoughtful."

Betina regained her composure. "It was the least I could do," Betina said, sitting down at the head of the table.

"Mmm, this is grand," Mr. Cambridge said when they'd begun eating. "I'd like to take this recipe home to my wife, if you wouldn't mind, Anna."

"No trouble at all, Mr. Cambridge. I'll be glad to write it down for you."

"Where did you learn to cook like this?" Betina asked.

"She's a chef," Mitch interjected.

"Oh? Where?" Mr. Cambridge asked.

"Celebración del Río in San Antonio," Anna said.

"You're kidding! I don't know how many times my wife and I've been there. Topnotch..." He looked at Betina, who was scowling at her perceived rival.

"Really topnotch," he finished quietly, then lifted an eyebrow and looked questioningly at Mitch.

Mitch seemed not to notice, the food on his plate disappearing at an alarming rate.

"I have more crêpes," Anna said to him. "May I get you some?"

Mitch smiled his approval, then handed his plate to her, and she was glad for the moment alone in the kitchen. The tense atmosphere she'd found in the living room had followed them into the dining room. Betina seemed ready to pounce, like a cat on a bird, and her intended victim was surely Mitchell. She'd told Anna earlier that she held a "handful of aces," and she'd, no doubt, been about to play the first one when Anna had interrupted them before dinner.

For some reason, Anna felt that Mitch was in some kind of danger. Her instincts were to protect him, but she had no idea how she might, nor any idea from what she would be protecting him. Aside from Betina's obvious goal, Mitch himself, Anna was positive that there was much more to it than that. Betina's reference to Mitch's responsibilities and "little Jess" had sounded threatening and ominous. That inner peace Anna had felt before the three had come back from the stables was now a disorganized jumble of contradictions.

She returned to silence. Instead of the steady flow of conversation that she'd left, no one was saying a word. Mitch thanked her and resumed eating his meal.

When she offered to refill Mr. Cambridge's plate, he declined, and she wasn't surprised. He was a slight man and hadn't struck her as a big eater. Betina was in the act of pouring herself more wine, and a curt "no, thanks" followed Anna's offer of more food.

Anna sat before her empty plate for a few more minutes, then pushed away from the table. "I'll go write down your recipe, Mr. Cambridge," she said. Then to Mitch, "I found a pad and pen in one of the kitchen drawers. May I use them?"

"Sure," he said. "Anything you want."

"Thanks."

"I'll come with you," Mr. Cambridge offered. "My wife never refuses help in the kitchen." He picked up his plate and wineglass, came around the table, and followed Anna out of the dining room.

"Mind if I rinse these dishes while you write?" he asked. "Kind of a payment for the recipe."

"I won't mind at all, Mr. Cambridge, but you don't owe me anything for this." She held up the pad she had. "I made it up just this evening from what I could find in here."

"Amazing," he said. "Uh, call me Hal, will you?"

"Of course...Hal."

Anna was still writing when he'd finished his rinsing. He excused himself and left the kitchen by way of the door to the living room. She heard the front door open and close, but didn't take the time to wonder where he was going. As she sat alone in the kitchen, she could hear Betina begin to speak in a low voice, but she couldn't understand the words she was saying. Neither could she understand Mitch's response. In a moment, though, the voices became louder, clearer, and angry.

"That's blackmail," Mitch said.

"I wouldn't call a paternity suit blackmail," Betina said.

"You can call it anything you like, but that's *exactly* what it is."

"It's either that, or Cabe Corner, Mitchell...or me."

"Threats aren't going to do you a bit of good, Mrs. Ogden."

"Don't call me that!"

"That's your name, isn't it?" Mitch asked.

"It's going to be Mrs. McCabe," Betina hissed.

"Over my dead body," Mitch countered.

"Or that of your son," Betina said bitterly.

Ten

Your son. Anna wanted to put her hands over her ears and block out the hateful sound of Betina's voice, but the last words she'd heard kept ringing through her mind. *Your son.*

She dropped the pen she held, fled from the kitchen, into the living room, and down the hall to the guest room. The door closed quietly behind her, she crossed to the corner chairs and sat down. In seconds she was on her feet, the lack of motion more than her body could stand.

The pacing didn't help either, but she kept it up, her mind reeling from the impact of an acerbic array of questions. Intuitively, Anna knew that Mitchell

McCabe was an honorable man, so it was almost impossible to believe that he'd abandoned a child to the sole care of its mother. The man she'd come to know and love just wouldn't be able to do such a thing.

But the facts stated otherwise. The hurt Anna felt could not be compared to any other she'd ever experienced. With little computation, it was obvious that Jess had been conceived over two years after Mitch and Betina were divorced. Their relationship had never really ended, and Anna felt somehow betrayed.

She stopped in the middle of the room and covered her face with her hands. *What am I thinking about?* she asked herself silently. Mitch was free to do exactly as he pleased. His partners in bed had nothing to do with her. Neither his ex-wife nor his son should be her concern. She took up her pacing again, this time with tears in her eyes. The conflict between Mitch and Betina was none of her business, but she still felt that he hadn't been able to trust her with the fact that he had a child of his own.

So the question was: Why hadn't he, at least, told her about Jess? Perhaps he'd thought she would have objected to his nonparental role. Maybe he viewed his relationship with Anna as such a brief affair that it seemed useless to share more than the most insignificant trivia. But that didn't ring completely true; he'd already told her so many things about his family. She felt as if she knew his Uncle Thomas's family fairly well without ever having seen them; she had more than passing knowledge of his father and mother and their home in Mimbres, New Mexico. He'd given her what she'd presumed to be an accurate history of his life without hesitation.

The one thing he *had* been reluctant to talk about was his marriage, she realized. It had seemed unfair to press him on the subject; the memories that might surface could be painful, and Anna hadn't wanted to hurt him in that way. From that first mention of the "bride he'd had once," Anna had left it alone unless he chose to mention it himself.

Anna sat down on the edge of the bed and tried to understand why Betina seemed like such a vengeful person. She was obviously well off, either because of her business dealings, or the divorce settlement, or both. She had a two-year-old child who should be filling her leisure time with great joy. She'd obviously met another man who loved her enough to marry her in spite of the fact that she carried Mitch's child.

Anna stood and began pacing again. From Joey's conversation with Mitch, Anna had gathered certain bits and pieces that startled her now that she'd had time to put the story together. At the time of her second marriage, Betina had been seeing Mitchell McCabe.

With paper and pen, Anna began to calculate from the snippets of information she'd heard from Ger-

maine, Mitch, and Joey. Eight years ago, Mitch had
married Betina and bought the two hundred acres now
known as Cabe Corner. Three years later they were
divorced. One year after that, Mitch had brought in
his first oil well, and within the next year or so, Betina
had tried to win back her ex-husband.

If Jess were exactly two years old, as Joey had said,
then Betina had gotten pregnant at almost exactly the
same time she'd gotten married for the second time.
Had Betina chosen Ogden because Mitch had finally
rejected her completely? Anna wondered. Had Mitch
been having second thoughts ever since their divorce
and given Betina reason to believe that they still had
a chance as husband and wife? Had Mitch wanted to
marry Anna to get away from Betina's heckling, or,
worse, his responsibilities to Jess?

Anna felt exhausted, the puzzle too complicated for
her tired mind. She wanted to move into action, pack
her suitcase, and leave Cabe Corner for good. In a
single smooth motion she was off the bed and had
her suitcase open on it. The first thing she lifted from
the drawer where she'd put her clothes was the red
nightgown, and she tossed it toward the bed. But the
impossibility of leaving struck her before the lush red
satin had fallen into the case. The spacious room
seemed to shrink, and the pleasant surroundings became a prison. She'd had too much of prisons!

Leaving the guest room seemed the answer to her

discomfort. In the darkened hallway, she could hear three voices now, and she assumed that Mr. Cambridge had returned. Instead of turning left toward the living room, she went straight ahead, her goal being to find another outside door and leave the cloistered feeling of the house for the refreshing coolness of the evening.

The house was much larger than it had appeared to be from the outside. Several rooms opened into the hall, but only two were lighted. She peeked into the first and found a room smaller than the guest room. A man's suit was neatly draped over a chair, a pair of dress shoes on the floor below it. Hal Cambridge's room, she decided, and she moved on toward the second light.

The room she entered at the end of the hall had to be the master bedroom. It was enormous and done in the most unusual furniture she'd ever seen. Bedposts, foot, and headboard of the huge bed were rough-cut logs, the bark still intact. Tables and chairs were of the same rugged design, and the whole of the room, complete with stone fireplace, appeared to be a remote mountain cabin standing apart and all to itself. After a moment of looking around, she spotted a door that appeared to open to the outside. As she crossed to it, something on the bed caught her eye, and she detoured near enough to see what it was.

The sheer, rust-colored material would have escaped unnoticed on the rust, tan, and brown of the bedspread if it hadn't been for the shimmering gold threads that ran through the bodice. The lace-trimmed teddy was almost transparent, the high-cut legs and thin straps making it seem almost too fragile to wear. But it wasn't designed to wear for long, Anna decided. It would be used for seduction and nothing else, then be discarded, in a most provocative way, no doubt.

Anna felt suddenly consumed by anger, an emotion she hadn't had to deal with for several hours. Compassion flew in the face of rage. Confusion disappeared, and in its place there was fury. None of it made any sense, but the tempest was real and simmering within her. There was no reasoning with it. The simple fact that Mitch would be out of her life forever in just a few days made no difference. The simple fact that she wanted no man in her life mattered not. The simple fact that Mitch had his own life to live meant nothing.

Mitch had brought her into this stormy den of battle on purpose, and she wanted no part of it. Incensed, and unable to fathom the reason for his deed, she hurried to leave the room.

The moment she set foot outside, she was in another world. The full moon overhead sent shafts of silver night through the leaves of the old trees. The fragrance of new grass and hay and sturdy animals gave the cool, spring air a lovely touch of elegance. Horses bade her hello with soft whickering, and a few greetings were whinnied in louder voices of welcome.

The stables could barely be seen through the many trunks and branches, but Anna started toward the sounds and soon reached the first white fence past the trees. Straight ahead, a wide, grassy paddock shone in the moonlight. To the left, the creek whispered its way to the west, and on the right a long, white stable extended the full length of the pasture.

She leaned on the fence, letting the calm of the night wash through her, and the cool air soothe her jittery stomach. Her anger would have to be stayed; her baby had to have a peaceful dwelling place. She would have to preserve her dignity by forgetting what was going on inside the house. It wouldn't be an easy task, but she was determined to do it. Turning, she rested her back against the fence and gazed at the house. At this moment, it seemed impossible that she'd actually given credence, even some consideration, to her musings about marriage to Mitch.

A shadow appeared on the shade in the room Anna had thought occupied by Mr. Cambridge. It faded, appeared again, and then the light was snapped off. Anna turned her back on the house that was so full of conflict. She preferred the uncomplicated company of these distant horses to the devious creatures inside that she'd met this day.

* * *

Mitch faced Betina for what he hoped would be the last time in his life—but it wasn't likely. She'd been pitiless in her accusations and recriminations, and she continued, even now, repeating endlessly, unmercifully. All Mitch wanted to do was to find out why Anna had left the kitchen and where she'd gone. He steadied himself for the last assault he was going to allow.

"I don't care how much you deny it, Jess is your child, and he's going to have you for his father," Betina was saying.

"I've never even seen the child, Betina. If this is true, and I don't believe it is, why didn't you tell me a long time ago?"

"I had my reasons," Betina said.

"And I'll tell you what they were. You knew it wouldn't wash then, just like you know it won't now. The child isn't mine, and that can be proven."

"Oh, dandy! You'd submit your own son to the pain of a blood test and the humiliation of a paternity suit."

"You're the heartless one, Betina. Don't try to put any of the blame for this on me."

"The blame stays where it belongs, and that's with one quick roll in the hay and an unlucky shot...if you'll forgive my metaphor."

"I'm not forgiving you anything. You've tried everything, even blackmail, to get me out of here and back into your bed. It isn't going to work, Betina."

"Not even if little Jess needs you?" she whined.

"He doesn't need me. He needs his father."

"Jess isn't well, Mitch."

"You're lying."

"Ask Joey," she said.

Mitch turned away from her and took a deep breath. "What's wrong with him?" he asked.

"I'm taking him to Dallas for tests tomorrow," Betina said.

"Send the bill to me," Mitch said without looking at her.

"Is that an admission of guilt?"

"No."

Her hands were on his arms, holding tightly. "I can't handle this alone, Mitch. I've got to have some help."

The desperation in her voice made him turn around. There were tears in her eyes. "Deceit isn't the way to get help, Betina," he said gently.

"But I need *more* than help—I need *you*, Mitch. I've *always* needed you."

"Is that why you walked out?" he asked.

"I've changed, you'll see. I'm not the same person who walked out on you."

"For one night, about three years ago, I thought that was true," he said.

Betina hung her head and wouldn't look at him.

Mitch knew why she was ashamed. She'd left his bed to go to her own wedding shower, but she hadn't known that he'd found out. All she knew was that he'd refused to see her the next day, the day before her wedding to Ogden. In a roundabout way, he'd forced her into the marriage by his rejection, but honestly and logically, he couldn't take the blame for that. It probably wouldn't have made any difference, but not once, in all the time she'd been trying to get him back, had she ever said "I love you."

"It's not going to end here, Mitch," she said.

"Yes, it is."

"You can't have Anna, I won't let you."

"She doesn't want me," he said softly.

Betina looked up in surprise. "You're wrong about that," she said.

"You never were very good about guessing how someone else felt," he said.

"How little you know about me," Betina said bitterly.

"Maybe that's true, but—"

"Then prepare yourself for a lesson, Mr. McCabe," she interrupted.

Mitch watched her walk away and disappear into the hallway. He knew that she didn't make idle threats. Whatever she had in mind, she would carry out, no matter whether it worked to her benefit or not.

A paternity suit might still be in his future. She'd
thought the threat of a suit would make him sell the
isolated home that she had always hated so that he
would be free to move in with her.

Poor Hal Cambridge. He hadn't known he was to
be a pawn in Betina's game. He'd left the living room
much relieved that Mitch had flatly refused his offer.
When he'd reappeared to say his goodbyes, Mitch had
made sure that Hal knew their arrangements concern-
ing Old Blue were still on. Hal had been grateful.

Now all Mitch wanted to do was to find Anna. He
went straight to the guest room and knocked on the
door, then knocked again when there was no answer.
He pushed the door open and looked inside. No one
was there, and he crossed the room and peeked into
the bathroom. Empty. On his way back to the door
he glanced at the bed and saw her suitcase. The
lustrous red material draped over it lured him forward.

He could hardly believe what he had in his hands.
The garment wasn't like anything Anna had ever
worn before. He spread the gown out on the bed and
ran his hand over it. It was almost as if he could feel
her lush body beneath the shimmering satin. As he
drew his hand back, he heard a slight disturbance
from the direction of the stables.

Just outside the guest room door, to the right, there
was a short, narrow hall that led to a back door. Mitch
hurried out. Forrest had told him about a pack of dogs

that had been running loose in the area, and he half
ran to the tack room at the near end of the stables.
Inside, he removed a shotgun from a rack and went
back outside. He heard the crack of a twig and moved
forward to investigate.

"I guess that's one way to get rid of unwanted
guests," Anna said when he came into sight.

"Anna! What are you doing out here?"

"Listening to your horses talk," she said easily,
then pointed at the gun. "But I didn't know it was a
punishable offense."

Mitch stood the weapon against a fence post and
took a step closer.

Anna took a step back. "I was just going in," she
said.

"May we talk first?" Mitch asked.

"I'd rather not," Anna said.

"I know you're upset. I don't blame you, but I'd
like to explain some things."

"I don't want to know any more than I do right
now," she said, then started to move away.

"I'm not selling the property," he said, following
her.

"I didn't think you would. It's a good place to
hide."

"From what?"

"Your responsibilities," she said.

"What do you mean?" he asked.

"Your son."

Mitch caught her arm and stopped her. "I don't have a son," he said.

"Betina believes otherwise."

"Betina is wrong."

"Are you saying there's no possibility that Jess is yours?" she asked, her anger returning.

He couldn't lie to her. "No," he said quietly.

"Then why do you persist in denying it?"

"Because the probability is almost zero."

"Now who's being naive?" Anna asked, and began to walk again.

Mitch stopped her a second time. "One night out of God knows how many she'd already spent with Ogden!" He hung his head, sighed, then looked up. "I fell for her story," he said apologetically. "I actually believed that she'd changed her mind about living out here, about enjoying the animals and the quiet and the isolation."

"But Jess could still be your son," Anna said.

"I suppose he could."

"Aren't you the least bit curious? Don't you want to know for sure?" Anna asked.

"Yes, and I intend to find out," he said. "But whatever happens, there will be no Betina in my life."

Anna moved toward the door of the master bedroom. "I'm going to say good-night now, Mitch. I'm very tired."

He wanted to mention the red nightgown, but the moment didn't seem right. He would give her time to get ready for bed, then knock on her door. Perhaps he could bring glasses of wine, maybe some chocolate he'd kept in his freezer since his last trip to Houston. More than anything else he wanted to hold her and tell her how sorry he was that she'd had to endure one of Betina's games. *Am I never to be free of this craziness?* he wondered, as Anna opened the door and stepped inside.

Anna took three or four steps into the room before she realized it was occupied. In the dim light of the far corner, Betina stood up from the chair she'd been sitting in. She wore nothing but the transparent teddy Anna had seen lying on the bed.

Anna averted her eyes. "Excuse me," she said, then got across the room and out the door as hastily as possible.

Mitch had been watching Anna, his eyes not wanting to leave her womanly shape and easy movements. He became aware of Betina's presence just seconds after Anna had spoken.

"What the hell—!"

"I told you I wouldn't let you have her," Betina said with a smile. "I didn't know she'd be so willing to help me."

"Get out of here," Mitch said, his voice rough with emotion.

"Didn't you hear me? I told you it wouldn't be finished here."

"You've finished more than you can imagine," he said. "I want you out of here—now!"

Eleven

Anna threw the suitcase and its delicate red contents to the floor, then fell across the bed. The tears she'd expected didn't come. Instead, her fists were tightly doubled, her jaw was clenched, and the muscles of her shoulders felt like knots. Unseeing eyes stared straight ahead as she lay prone across the bright yellow spread.

She couldn't identify the emotion she was feeling. It seemed to be a sickening combination of anger, disgust, anguish, and loss. Never before had she felt such distress. The embarrassment of walking in on the nearly naked Betina had furnished enough discomfort to last a lifetime all by itself. The possibility of Mitch's having a child tormented her. But still there were no tears.

Anna suddenly rolled over and sat up in the middle of the bed, her legs crossed Indian fashion. *Who the devil am I kidding?* she asked herself pointedly. *And how many times do I have to go over this before I get it straight in my head?* She'd walked into the relationship with her eyes wide open. Though her facts hadn't been in perfect order, she'd accepted her own terms and made an emotional commitment to only one thing, a life with her baby.

It was all the vacillating back and forth that had confused her so. One minute she'd think that being a single parent was the most wonderful thing that could happen to her. The next minute she'd be thinking how nice it would be to have Mitch around all the time, just as if the choice were completely up to her.

Now, here at Cabe Corner, she'd found that his life was so mixed up and bogged down in one tribulation after another that he'd not really had any choices of his own. Mitchell McCabe was not truly a free man. So be it, she decided, as she got off the bed and went into the bathroom. That made everything blissfully simple.

Then why wasn't she feeling blissful? she wondered, as she undressed and stepped into the shower. The warm water eased her tension somewhat, while she examined the facts of her present existence. She was more in charge of her life than either Betina or Mitch. She would be making all the decisions from now on. No one would be telling her what she could or couldn't do. Only her baby would be allowed to dictate. Just thinking about the tiny spark of life growing within her was exhilarating. It was all she'd ever wanted, she thought, as she stepped out of the shower.

She'd never needed someone to dream about, never yearned for a frilly, traditional relationship. The anxieties of dating had been less than appreciated. Real romance seemed too fragile to exist in everyday life. Love seemed capricious, at best. Only the baby was real, and she now had everything she'd ever wanted. She stood in the doorway wondering what to put on, when she saw the red nightgown on the floor across the room.

Not that, she decided, and thought about pressing it into a scrapbook. The idea made her smile as she donned her full-length, faithfully modest robe. The sound of a car engine drew her toward the window. Betina's Mercedes shone bright silver in the moonlight as it sped, northbound, along the creek road. She watched until the car disappeared, then continued to stare out at the silent night wondering if Mitch had left with her. The quiet knock on the door startled her.

"What is it?" she asked, hurrying to secure the sash of the robe.

"Room service," came the reply.

"Whatever you're selling, we don't want any." The words were out before she'd thought about them, and brought back memories of their first conversation through their adjoining door at La Maison.

"I just wanted to apologize," he said.

He hadn't forgotten, either. That's exactly the way he'd answered her father's silly greeting before. The familiar history felt comfortable, and, for some reason, she wanted to keep it going. "Shouldn't you be getting some sleep?" she asked, and wondered if he'd remember what he'd said before. He did...and he didn't.

"I was just headed that way," he said, as he had before. "But I didn't want to go alone," he revised.

"Mitch—"

"Anna, I want to talk to you."

Anna moved toward the door. "I'm very tired, Mitch."

"I won't keep you. I understand."

But of course he didn't understand, and she couldn't bring herself to tell him through a closed door. It would sound so crass and unnatural in any circumstance—*your services are no longer needed.* "Come in, Mitch," she said finally.

Mitch opened the door, but he didn't step inside. Just as he'd appeared at her door on her first night at La Maison, he held a tray with two glasses and a bottle of wine. Anna couldn't believe that he'd remembered so well.

"I thought you might like a little brandy before bed."

"Come in."

"I have a fire going in the other room," he said.

"Mitch..." she started to protest.

"Please."

"Still the persuasive type," she said with a slight smile, then stepped past him and turned toward the living room.

"This way," Mitch said, taking her arm.

Anna resisted. "I wouldn't be comfortable in there," she said.

Mitch kissed her temple. "She's never slept in that room. I added it on after she left," he said.

She was inordinately pleased, but she didn't know why. Betina had nothing to do with Anna's destiny. "All right," she said.

In the light of the blazing fire, the room looked even more rustic than it had before. Happily, there was no evidence that the other woman had ever been there. Anna sat down in the chair Mitch indicated and watched him pour two small portions of brandy into the snifters. The warmth from the fire felt good, and she was pleasantly surprised, as he handed her the wine, that the room caused her no discomfort.

Mitch sat down, leaned his head back, then looked

over at her. "I'm glad this day is over, aren't you?" he asked.

It sounded as if they'd been through the problems together and overcome them as a couple. "Very glad," Anna said.

"I'm sorry about all the uproar," he said quietly.

Anna's heart went out to him. He'd expected none of what had happened. "What will you do, Mitch?" she asked.

"Tonight, nothing. All I want to do is be with you. You have no idea how much that means to me right now. In all my life, I've never been so comfortable with anyone."

It shocked her that he needed her emotional support; he'd always seemed so self-sufficient. He'd admitted that he'd never allowed someone else to determine the circumstances of his life, as she had. Now the tables were turned; Betina's accusations had changed all that.

"Is there anything I can do to help you?" she asked.

"Just being here with me is enough. Just looking at you makes me happy." He leaned forward. "You're so beautiful in the firelight, Anna. Remember the first time we sat in front of a fire?"

"Very well," she said, slightly embarrassed. That night had been the beginning of an intimacy she'd never imagined.

"I'll remember that night forever," he said quietly. "And every other minute we've spent together."

"So will I, Mitch." She looked away from him. *The baby will be a constant reminder for me,* she thought, *and he'll have nothing but memories.*

Mitch put his glass down, got up, then knelt to one side of her crossed legs. "I want you to know that I'll always be here for you. If you ever need anything, all you have to do is ask."

This goodbye sounded so final. Anna returned her brandy to the table and lifted his hand from the arm of the chair. She brought it to her cheek and rubbed the back of it against her skin. "You're a kind person," she said, then held his hand in both of hers.

"There isn't anything I wouldn't do for you, Anna. You know that, don't you?"

"Yes."

"I know it hasn't been a pleasant stay, but thank you for coming home with me," he said.

"I'm glad I got to see Cabe Corner. It fits you perfectly."

Mitch leaned forward and took her face in his hands. "You make it feel like a home," he said, then lightly kissed her.

Anna couldn't help herself; her arms went around him and pulled him closer. She wanted to feel the touch of his mouth again, to feel the pressure of his legs against hers. The kiss was like a drug, an addictive contentment that could be replaced by nothing else. He tasted of aromatic wine, his lips a delicious gift of pleasure. She felt the now familiar warmth of desire curl within her, and she could barely believe that it would still be possible now that her dream had been fully realized.

"Oh, Mitch. I'm so sorry for what you've been through today," she whispered next to his cheek, thinking to bring her mind back to reality.

"Being with you is all that matters to me right now, Anna."

She pulled his head to her breast and smoothed the black hair that curled toward his ears. It felt so good to hold him, to try to comfort him. "I just wish there was something more I could do to help you get through this," she said softly.

He pulled away from her. "There is," he said. "Wait right here."

Anna remained composed and calm until he returned. As soon as he walked in the door with the red nightgown in his hand, her self-possession evaporated. Only moments ago, before he'd knocked at her door, she'd been sure that she would never put the garment on.

He held it out to her. "You can model this for me," he said.

"Mitch, I…"

"I wish I'd bought it for you, but I wasn't sure

you'd…'' He took her hand and pulled her up to face him. "You bought this yourself, didn't you?"

Anna nodded slowly.

"After we…?"

She nodded again.

"Please put it on."

Anna closed her eyes briefly. She couldn't say no to him. "Where?" she asked softly.

He pointed to a door across the room.

Once the gown was on, she hesitated to leave the spacious bath. The full-length mirror on the wall reflected a person Anna didn't know. Already, her breasts felt larger, and the deep V of the neckline seemed barely able to contain her. The shimmering material molded her body as a second skin, and the high, off-center slit up the straight skirt seemed to promise a seductive invitation. The image of the sensual woman she saw unnerved her. But even as she stood there, debating the intelligence of her return to the bedroom, she could feel his strong hands on her body, and she knew that she wasn't ready for it to end.

When she opened the door, she saw that he'd been busy while she was gone. A single candle, she hadn't noticed until now, was lighted on one of the nightstands, the bed was turned down, and his boots stood on the hearth. He was looking into the fire, holding his snifter of brandy, his back to her. She closed the door as quietly as she could, but, somehow, he knew she was there and turned around.

She heard his sharp intake of air as she moved toward him, then a long sigh as he put his glass down on the table. His eyes followed every step as she approached, his admiration plain. Standing before him was one of the hardest things she'd ever done.

"This is the nicest gift anybody's ever given me," he said softly. His finger eased under one of the thin straps and moved back, then forward. "You surprise me endlessly."

"Me, too," she said.

He smiled. "Why did you buy this, Anna?"

She looked into the fire. "For you," she said honestly.

"And that surprises you?" he asked.

"Yes."

"But you look so beautiful. That would be reason enough to buy it."

"I haven't ever felt like…"

"Like a beautiful woman?" he asked. "Like a desirable woman?" His hands described what he saw, as his words whispered to her. "How could you think of yourself otherwise?" He touched the sides of her breasts, his palms pressing lightly inward. "A madonna in red," he said softly. "You blossom like a flower in my hands, Anna."

She savored his touch and felt the sensitive skin of

her bosom pressing tighter against the smooth fabric. Without looking, she knew that the tips of her breasts were straining against the satin, the sensation quickening her pulse. Even completely nude, she'd never felt so exposed, so acutely revealed.

Two fingers started at the bottom of the plunging neckline, then moved lightly up each side of the wide V. "You flatter the gown, Anna. No one else could do so much for it." His hands descended to cup her breasts, and he bowed his head to kiss the rounded curves he lifted.

When he looked up, she wrapped her arms around him and pulled him closer, wanting to feel his body against hers. "Hold me," she murmured. His hands on her bare back felt hard and strong. She knew his hands well; they had touched every part of her, captivated her, and turned her will to his. Her own had never ventured so far, never been so bold.

The idea of exploring, as he had, inflamed her. She began to tremble as the impelling thought prompted her hands to tug at the back of his shirt. When it was free, they moved to the front and performed the same task.

"Anna?"

"Shh!" She couldn't risk being distracted or she might lose her nerve. Before they parted, she had to know the magic of him completely. Each button yielded to deliberate fingers, and his shirt was soon lying in a heap on one of the chairs. Her hands brushed over his chest, studying every appeal, every enticing contour. With deliberate strokes, she outlined the pattern of black hair that adorned the wide expanse of muscled flesh. Then her hands moved to his hips.

Blue denim hugged him tightly, and she could feel the solid bones of his thighs against the palms of her hands. She hesitated, wondering if she had the courage to continue. As if he had read her mind, he took her hand and led her to the side of the bed. As he had always done, he would take over now, knowing that her shyness would prevent her from crossing some invisible boundary.

But she surprised him. Instead of melting into his arms, she steadied herself with her hands against his shoulders, then relinquished her hold to begin unfastening his belt. The five buttons of his Levi's gave her a slight problem, but she purposefully refused his help.

"Not this time, Mitch," she said softly.

Not giving herself time to consider, she knelt as she pulled at the trousers and briefs, making only the concession of closing her eyes until she knew she'd passed his knees. He obligingly stepped out of the two garments. Then she tugged his socks off one at a time. Again she hesitated. What madness had assailed her? she wondered, but the sight of his long, hair-roughened legs tempted her even as she questioned her sanity.

She was lured to touch him, and as she rose, her hands trailed up the outside of his legs. Oh, how she wanted to explore farther, to touch the force that had given her such pleasure these weeks past.

Mitch covered her hands with his and guided them around his waist. He drew her close. "Is it the red gown that gives you this new courage?" he whispered.

"It's you," she said.

"I'm honored."

"You deserve so much," she said.

"You've already given me—"

"Not enough," she said, and leaned against him.

He picked her up, turned, and laid her gently on the bed. As she moved over, he eased down beside her, but before he could take her into his arms again, she was on her knees next to him.

"Let me look at you." She put a hand on his chest, then began to lower it, her eyes following its descending course. "Your body is beautiful," she said, glancing at his face, wavering in her determination. But her searching hand didn't falter, and when it reached its destination, his eyes shone in sweet agony.

He'd given her everything she wanted, and love besides. She returned his love, but she wanted to give him more. "Tell me how to please you," she said softly.

He breathed her name, "Anna…" Then he gasped as her hand closed over him.

The sound frightened her. Her hand moved to safer terrain on his hard stomach, but she was determined to return to that sacred place. Her kisses started at his lips. "I want to touch you like you've touched me," she murmured next to his cheek, then nibbled at his jaw. Her lips closed over the lobe of his ear, edged upward, her tongue tasting, sampling. "I want to kiss you like you've kissed me," she said softly into his ear.

She felt one strap of her gown being pulled down, but she couldn't be deterred. Her mouth moved to his neck, then to his shoulder, and she nipped at the smooth skin. The fragrance of some spicy soap clung to his body, making every new visit as enticing to inhale as to taste. Preoccupied with the tantalizing feel of his nipple beneath her tongue, she didn't notice that he'd succeeded in lowering the other strap.

As she moved over him, the crisp hair on his chest grazed against her bare bosom. She let out a sigh of pleasure, and regretted, for a fleeting moment, that she'd never been as brave as he. Her body was raging with desire as she covered his flat stomach with gentle kisses. And then she dared to touch him again, her hand moving deliberately this time, caressing, learning.

A deep moaning sound filled the quiet room, and a shiver of anticipation ran through her. The sound might have been her own; it had happened before. He'd given her so much pleasure, his kisses discovering her passion as she wanted to discover his.

"Anna..." His exclamation was released as a sobbing sound when her lips touched him for the first time. His hand skimmed her hair, then moved to her cheek, and he could feel her mouth touching him. He thought he might die if his heart were to beat any faster. He moved to pull her toward him.

"My love," he said, as he lowered her to the bed.

"I want you," she said urgently.

He couldn't wait to remove her gown. Instead, he pushed the soft satin up until it was gathered about her waist. His body trembled so, he didn't know if he would be able to support his own weight as he moved over her. But he needn't have worried. She clutched him to her breast, holding him as tightly as she could until the emptiness was gone, until the passion she'd kissed had fulfilled the impatient hunger within her.

Her eagerness astounded her, as she lifted to meet each thrust. She gasped for breath and rejoiced at the almost unbearable release that flooded her body with pleasure.

No other man would ever touch her, no other man

would ever enter her life. She would be so proud to carry this man's child, so grateful for his unselfish gift of paradise. Her heart would never say goodbye.

"I love you, Mitchell McCabe."

Twelve

Anna sat on the plane alone, the keys to Mitch's car in her purse, and her instructions to call Don to tell him he had the rest of the gig with The Pecos Tide carefully written in her pocketbook calendar. Sandy had landed at the Dallas-Fort Worth airport after half an hour in the holding pattern, and Mitch had gotten off. He was going to Parkland Hospital to be with Jess through the trials of his medical tests.

She could still see the strain on Mitch's face, still feel the anxiety he'd conveyed in his explanation and his short, nervous goodbye. He would see the boy for the first time today, the child that could be his son. Anna had volunteered to go with him, but he'd declined her offer, and she understood his need to face his future alone. She would be doing the same.

Their morning had been pleasant. Mitch had given her the tour he'd promised, and Anna had thoroughly enjoyed meeting all the horses as she helped with the morning chores. She'd also met Drex and the other young boy who were both apprenticed to Mitch as novice farriers, and she'd even gotten to witness the master at work.

The mysteries of tempering steel, and the running dialogue on the psychology and physiology of horses fascinated her, as she watched a loose shoe being re-shaped and replaced. The boys assisted in expert fash-ion, handing tools and following orders, as Mitch pared, trimmed, and rasped the hoof. His hammer blows were delivered with lightning speed, and the nail points twisted off with ease. The shoe was rasped smooth, and the hoof let down before the horse had a chance to get anxious.

It was yet another beautiful image to be cataloged and stored for remembering—the glow from the forge on the angles of his face, the powerful muscles of his bare arms and chest delivering blows to the incan-descent iron that made showers of star-sparks fly from his hammer, the soothing, caring words that created a calm rapport with the huge animal he lovingly tended. All would be filed away, but always and for-ever ready to be viewed again and again.

* * *

Mitch couldn't remember ever feeling so ill at ease as he did when he walked into Parkland Hospital. He was directed to pediatrics, then told by a nurse that Mrs. Ogden and her son were in an examining room with the doctor. The waiting area felt like a detention cell as he paced the tiled floor. He had just about decided to walk in on the examination uninvited, when another man entered the small room.

The tall, blond man sat down, then stood and walked to a window. He ran his hands through his hair, then turned to Mitch. "I hate this waiting," he said. "Makes me so damned nervous."

Mitch nodded. "I know how you feel," he said, but he knew he really didn't. He'd never had a child to care about as this man probably had.

"What takes these people so long?" The man took a cigarette from his shirt pocket, lit it, and inhaled deeply. In the same motion, he stubbed it out in the ashtray. "Sorry. Forgot where I was for a minute." He rubbed his hands together in nervous agitation. "Hospital's no place for smoking," he said.

"Hospitals make me nervous, too," Mitch said kindly.

The man thrust his hand toward Mitch. "Name's Ogden," he said. "Ray Ogden."

Mitch was so shocked he almost didn't take the

man's hand. "Mitchell McCabe," he said finally, grasping the thin hand in his.

Ray Ogden held on to Mitch's hand. "The hell, you say!" He smiled. "Well, I'll be damned. I never thought we'd meet."

Ray was still shaking his head when Mitch pulled his hand away.

"What a coincidence! Both of us here with a sick child at the same time," Ray went on. "Damned doctors! Keep you guessing and worrying." Ray put a hand on Mitch's shoulder. "Everything's going to be all right with yours, isn't it?" he asked seriously.

"I hope so," Mitch said.

"Jess has 'em puzzled, I guess. Been here all morning. Betina gets a little crazy about stuff like this...probably has them checking every hair on his head." Ray frowned. "I've been out of town. Just found out last night. Suppose you know that Betina and I are divorced."

"Yes, I knew," Mitch said softly.

Ray turned and stared out the window. "It's been tough...not being with little Jess. They grow up so fast...you miss so much. It's hard."

Mitch could hear the love Ray Ogden had for the child, and couldn't help but envy him. He felt as if he should leave, let the man go on believing that Jess was his son. But he couldn't. He had to know the truth and accept some of the responsibility if the child were his.

Now that he'd met Ray Ogden, his plan would have to be somewhat revised, however. Mitch could not bring himself to hurt the man if he could possibly avoid it. He would meet the child and simply introduce himself as a friend of the family. An open invitation to visit Cabe Corner would be extended, an anonymous trust fund set up, and an agreement with Betina would be made to assure Ray Ogden's parental status. The inquiry about the child's blood type would have to be discreetly made.

He looked at the man's back and could see the tension in the set of his shoulders. It all seemed so clinical and cold. Children should bring joy and warmth into the world, not bitterness and subterfuge. Perhaps Anna had been right to want to guard her relationship with her child, he thought despondently. Perhaps her decision was the more logical one given the present state of the world and its inhabitants' crazy preoccupation with temporary pleasures.

"Daddy!"

Mitch turned to see a slender two-year-old with a mass of blond ringlets toddle into the room. Ray Ogden rushed to him and lifted the slight child into his arms.

"Hey, there, tiger," Ray said, hugging the boy tightly to him.

The resemblance between them was remarkable, right down to the bright blue eyes, narrow face, and thin nose, and Mitch stood completely speechless while he watched a playful exchange of tickles and kisses. Betina must have been desperate for emotional support to have gone through with the charade he'd witnessed yesterday, he decided. She'd always been one to overreact to any stressful situation unless it had to do with her real estate business. In that arena, she could be more level-headed and businesslike than anyone Mitch had ever known.

Betina stood just outside the door talking to the doctor. "The tests were quite thorough, Mrs. Ogden," Mitch heard the doctor say to her. "I assure you, Jess is going to be just fine."

"Are you absolutely sure?" Betina asked anxiously.

The doctor nodded and placed a reassuring hand on her shoulder. "Now that you know what this little virus can do, you won't be nearly so upset the next time he comes down with a touch of the flu, Mrs. Ogden. And don't be afraid to take him to the doctor there in Kermit. Dr. Bently is extremely capable. He can easily handle this kind of problem. We'll just get these prescriptions filled out, and you can be on your way."

The relief on Ray's face was like a streak of sunshine, as he watched Betina move away from the door to accompany the doctor to the nurses' station. Mitch stepped toward him and extended his hand. "I've got to go talk to one of the nurses," he said, as he shook the man's hand. "I'm glad everything's okay with Jess…and I'm glad we finally got to meet."

"Good luck, Mitchell," Ray said sincerely. "Say bye-bye to Mr. McCabe, Jess." He lifted the boy's hand and waved.

"Bye-bye, Mitu Mabe," the boy said.

Betina's startled look when she saw him told Mitch that she hadn't been aware of his presence in the waiting room. He approached her with caution, ready for some sort of an outburst, but she surprised him.

She turned from the counter to face him. "I'm sorry, Mitch," she said simply. "I don't expect you to understand or condone my behavior."

"I think I understand, anyway," Mitch said. "I'm glad everything's all right with Jess," he added.

"Thanks. Does Ray know why you—?"

"No."

Betina sighed. "We're going to try it again. Did he tell you?"

"No, but he loves you, Betina."

"Yes…he does. And he loves his son, too." She looked down, then held her chin high. "We'll make it this time," she said.

"I wish you the very best, Betina."

She caught his arm as he started to move away.

"Tell Anna I'm sorry. I was so upset with…everything…Ray…my mother…"

"You don't have to explain," Mitch said and smiled. "I know your mother."

Betina nodded, then gave his arm a squeeze. "Thank you, Mitchell."

The next few days, the last with Pep Gutierrez, were busy ones. Every evening Anna would find a note on her door telling her that she had received a phone call from Mitch, and every night she would return the call. There was never an answer. She finally resorted to asking Germaine if she'd talked to him.

"That man!" Germaine's tone was one of exasperation. "Acts like he's too busy to give me the time of day. I guess you could say I've talked to him, but he just jabbers on about buying some fool airplane, and fixing up the hay barn so Drex can sleep over, and 'Where's Anna?' Always wanting to know, 'Where's Anna?'"

"Has he…said anything about…Betina?" Anna asked hesitantly.

"That's the strangest part. I'd reckon he hasn't even mentioned her name for the past five years." She paused and thought a minute. "I guess he did say something about her getting married again…but then Joey said she divorced the man."

"And the strangest part?" Anna reminded her.

"Oh, yes, well…Mitch is telling me all about how Betina and her ex-husband are getting back together, and what a beautiful blond-haired son they have. I think his name is Jess…or something like that. Anyway, Mitch couldn't be happier for them, and he made a trip all the way to Kermit to take the child a toy. Said the boy was getting over the flu."

She looked at Germaine, her black hair and brown eyes more beautiful than Anna could have imagined. Surely, Jess could not be Mitch's son. "If he calls again would you give him a message for me?"

"I'd be glad to," Germaine said.

"Tell him I'm leaving New Orleans early tomorrow morning. Tell him that I'll be calling him tomorrow night." She paused. "And tell him that I *expect* him to be waiting by the phone for my call. I have good news."

Germaine smiled. "You know? I think he'll like taking orders from you. God knows, that man needs some direction in his life. Some good news won't hurt him, either."

Anna was packed and ready to go by three in the morning. Interstate 10 was practically deserted until she neared Lake Charles. From that point on, she kept her comfortable sedan even with the flow of traffic. By one o'clock in the afternoon she was entering the outskirts of San Antonio.

* * *

Mitch had gotten Anna's message from Germaine at ten the next morning, and the minutes to sunset had dragged by like years. He'd scrambled himself some eggs for his dinner but had left them sitting on the kitchen table, untouched, vowing to have a phone put in the kitchen as soon as the sun rose tomorrow morning.

He hovered near the phone in the bedroom, commending his good sense on having Drex move into the quickly remodeled hay barn so that the young man could look after the horses and prevent further problems. He alternately cursed and gave thanks. His initial plan, to return to New Orleans immediately, had been thwarted, first by an accident in the stables resulting in two injured horses, then by the illness of Forrest. He almost wished that he hadn't phoned from the hospital to find out how things were going.

At least he could be grateful that Anna had said she would call him. She'd said he was a persuasive man. He intended to use every trick he could think of to persuade her to let him come to San Antonio. If that didn't work, he was going anyway. Everything was set up for an extended stay. Drex understood his duties and would be well paid to take care of Cabe Corner for as long as necessary. Until Anna became pregnant, he wondered, or until he convinced her to marry him?

"Both, by damned!" he vowed aloud.

When the phone rang, Mitch jumped out of his chair and grabbed the receiver. "Anna?"

"Forrest," came the reply. "Just want to let you know that my boy will be over on Saturday to help Drex."

Mitch took a deep breath and tried to control his shaking hand. "Glad to hear it, Forrest. You all right?"

"Gettin' better," Forrest said.

"Well, thank you for calling."

He felt bad about hanging up on the man so quickly. He'd have to explain later. Eight o'clock passed in silence, as did nine, then ten. By ten-thirty, Mitch caught himself dozing in front of the fire, exhausted by the stress of waiting. His head fell, again, to his chest as the fire crackled before him and the mantel clock chimed eleven.

His dream took him to New Orleans, to the parlor of La Maison. Anna stood in front of a blazing fire, her silhouette a dark and sensuous form, her seductive curves an irresistible lure. She knelt before him, reaching out to touch his cheek, tempting him into wakefulness. She leaned forward, and he could feel the ripe fullness of her breasts against him. Her lips were touching his.

"Anna!"

"I'm here," she said.

"You didn't call," he said sleepily.

"I came home, instead."

"Your father must be glad to see you."

"He was," she said, smiling, realizing that Mitch was still half asleep.

"I'm coming for you, Anna. Tell your father that I'm going to marry you."

"I've already told him," she said proudly. For the first time in her life she'd felt in complete control of her destiny.

Mitch focused his eyes on the dream-woman kneeling before him. "Anna?"

"Yes?"

"I was just dreaming…"

"It wasn't a dream."

He gathered her into his arms, and the warmth of her body brought reality into sharp focus. "Yes, it was, my love. A dream come true."

Epilogue

"There he is! Come on!"

Mitch looked down at the five-year-old bundle of energy who was tugging at his finger. "Take it easy there, cowboy. Let's wait for your mother."

"They're too slow," the child moaned. "Santa Claus will fly away."

"Let's look for them, okay, partner?" Mitch lifted Josh and settled him on his shoulders, then gazed out over the throng of Christmas shoppers in San Antonio's North Star Mall.

"I see them!" Josh shouted, pointing. "Momma! Maria! Hurry up!"

"Good work, Josh," Mitch complimented. "See? We didn't have to wait long."

Josh started wiggling, impatient to get down and take his place in the line of children waiting to see Santa Claus. Mitch put him down and watched the boy hurtle himself toward the opening in the white picket fence nearby. He was already in an animated conversation with the boy ahead of him when Anna approached.

"Nothing shy about him," Anna said, smiling. Then she looked at the child she held in her arms. Maria's eyes were wide with awe and wonder as she stared at the jolly man in the red velvet suit.

"What do you think?" Mitch asked.

"I think she's ready," Anna said. "Did you pay the photographer?"

He nodded. "They can go up together. She might feel more comfortable that way."

"Good idea," Anna said. "Maria?" The girl kept staring straight ahead as another child was lifted onto Santa's lap. "Maria?" Anna said again.

Mitch looked at Anna and shrugged. This was their fifth Christmas spent in San Antonio with Anna's family, and they'd both hoped that Maria would, at least, approach the man so they could take a picture home for the rapidly filling photo albums.

"I want a fire engine," Maria said suddenly, her eyes still locked on Saint Nicholas.

Mitch smiled. "You'll have to tell Santa Claus," he said.

"Okay."

Anna and Mitch exchanged looks of surprise, as Maria began to push against her mother's shoulder.

"Hey!" Josh said loudly, as his sister stepped in front of him. "Momma!"

A stern look from Mitch instantly wiped the anger from his son's face. "I don't think we have to worry about Maria being shy, either," Mitch said.

They watched as Maria allowed Santa to lift her onto his knee. For just an instant the girl glanced in the direction of her parents, her delicate eyebrows peaking apprehensively. Just as quickly, she composed herself.

"I want a fire engine, and two balloons, and..."

"I guess three is the magic age," Mitch said.

"I was much older," Anna said.

"What?" Mitch gazed down at his wife, a puzzled look on his face.

"Before I started making my own decisions," Anna added.

The smile in his eyes spread across his face. "No regrets?" he asked.

"One," Anna said seriously.

His expression changed to concern. "One?"

"I wish I'd met you ten years earlier," she said.

Mitch sighed in relief and slipped his arm around her waist. "We'll just have to live ten years longer than we planned to," he said.

"Make that twenty, and you've got a deal, cow-boy."

"You're the boss. Twenty, it is."

Anna nestled closer. "We'll have plenty to do."

"How's that?" Mitch asked, distracted momentar-ily by the flash of light from the photographer's bulb.

"Three children will keep us busy," Anna said qui-etly.

"Two children," he corrected, then quickly looked at her. "Three?"

"Christmas surprise," she said.

He pulled her closer. "And another dream come true," he whispered.

* * * * *

SILHOUETTE *Romance*

Escape to a place where a kiss is still a kiss...
Feel the breathless connection...
Fall in love as though it were
the very first time...
Experience the power of love!

Come to where favorite authors——such as
*Diana Palmer, Stella Bagwell,
Marie Ferrarella* and many more——
deliver heart-warming romance and genuine
emotion, time after time after time....

Silhouette Romance——
stories straight from the heart!

Silhouette®
Where love comes alive™